Without a Care

Ivory Dogan
Dalya B. Johnson
Heidi Mercado
Charlotte Marshall Murray
Yvonne Hernández
Rashonda Jones Aiken
Kim Carrington
Sonya Felice Jenkins

P.O. Box 402
Swiftwater, PA 18370
(973) 348-5067
sspublishingcompany@gmail.com
www.sharsheypublishingcompany.com

Copyright © 2019 Shar-Shey Publishing Company LLC
ISBN: 13: 978-0-9997922-7-8
ISBN: 10: 0-9997922-7-X
Book Cover Designed by: Dynasty's Visionary Designs
Edited by: ATW Editing

All rights reserved by the authors, who are the sole copyright owners of their stories in this anthology. No part of this book may be reproduced or transmitted in any form or by any means, electronic or mechanical, including photocopying, recording, or by any information storage and retrieval system, without permission in writing from the copyright owner. This book was printed in the United States of America.

Table of Contents

Heart Over Matter (Ivory Dogan)

A Forbidden Love (Dalya B. Johnson)

Rising From Defeat (Heidi Mercado)

The Other Side of Karma (Charlotte Marshall Murray)

A Chosen Life (Yvonne Hernández)

My Husband, Her Ex (Rashonda Jones Aiken)

The Heat of the Sun (Kim Carrington)

A Gift From Love (Sonya Felice Jenkins)

Acknowledgments (Sharnel Williams, C.E.O.)

Heart Over Matter

By

Ivory Dogan

Ivory Dogan

Ivory Dogan was born and raised in Jersey City, NJ. She's a lover of God and credits Him as the reason she lives today. After turning 30 years old six months ago, she has hit the ground running ever since! Ivory has always had the gift of writing, whether it be poetry, creative writing, rap freestyles, speeches, etc. Creating has always been a passion. With her children watching her every move, she vows to make them proud and clear the path for them to be great!

Heart Over Matter

Gracie was awakened by her alarm. She groggily turned on her side to smash the snooze button. Then it hit her. "Today is the day!" she said aloud. In one swift motion, she popped up out of bed, put her well-manicured pink toes into her furry Steve Madden slippers, and headed for her bathroom. She turned on the shower and kept walking to her closet. "I want my outfit to scream sophistication but whisper sexy," she said to herself, scanning her rack of clothing. Just then, her eyes landed on her all black, long sleeve, peplum waist dress by Donna Karen. "See! Mema is wrong about me!" Gracie said, feeling vindicated. "She says I shop too much?! No! I say, my spirit just tells me what I need before I need it!" Gracie laughed to herself as she headed toward the steamy shower.

AS WE LAY WITHOUT A CARE

As the hot water rolled off of Gracie's body, she fell into deep thought. An overwhelming feeling of gratitude had come over her. "Thank you, Lord," she mouthed as she thought about how her life had come full circle. Just two years ago, she'd lost the love of her life. For a long time, Gracie was brokenhearted and severely depressed. With that, her whole life crumbled right before her eyes. She dropped out of grad school, moved back in with her mom (which she refers to as Mema) unemployed and unmotivated. With the help of God, a praying mother, and peaceful solitude (no social media) she was able to dig herself out of that rut.

She put her inner forearm under the shower stream to allow the soap to rinse, to get a glimpse of the tattoo her and Mema got together to emancipate Grace's new journey to life. On Gracie's arm it read: "Isaiah 5/4/17" and Mema's read: "Roman 8/28." So, no matter where she goes, or what she does, she remembers who brought her this far. She looked up at the clock. "OMG, I'm going to be late if I don't hurry." She bathed, dried, and moisturized herself in 40 minutes flat. She put on the black dress and admired how it fit. Not snug, but her curves were visible. The peplum always set off her shape. Grace had caramel-colored skin and long straight hair down her back. Everyone says she gets her hair grade from Mema. She was thick with nice hips. Her bowed legs are similar to the actress Nia Long. And she had one dimple on the right cheek. She slid into her black Giuseppe pumps, put on cranberry-colored matte lipstick, and unwrapped her black hair with honey colored streaks. Satisfied with her look, she did a swirl in the mirror once more and sprayed on her Dolce perfume. She grabbed her truck keys and headed to the alarm panel to arm it before she left. She hit the key to her Mercedes truck, hopped in and drove off.

The 'Steak-Out'

June sat in his black SUV, munching on nacho cheese Doritos. "Man this ain't nothing like those steak-outs I used to see on TV," he said with crumbs falling out of his mouth. He took a swig of water and reached for his half smoked weed blunt. "I don't even know why they call it a steak-out, a nigga can't even get a steak!" June said while inhaling the strong-smelling ganja. He couldn't help but laugh at himself. Just then, his marijuana trivia was interrupted by his subject leaving the house. He continued to smoke on his blunt, as he watched her hit the alarm to her black Benz truck. "And to think, in just a few weeks all that beauty gonna be six feet under some dirt." June laughed to himself as he took another pull. "And who even made up the rule of being six feet under anyway?" he said as he continued to laugh. The sound of his phone ringing broke his concentration.

"Wassup B? What that situation looking like?" the caller questioned.

"Same ole' same ole'. Out the door at 7:55, armed and secured, expected to resurface at 4:55," June managed to say. "Okay bet! Moves in motion."

"Hit me if anything" the caller said before hanging up.

Watching the same person for so long, June was just as invested as Phifer.

Phifer MacCall

As Phifer hung up the phone, he couldn't help the satisfaction he felt. The woman who was responsible for his brother's death was finally going to pay. The person who actually pulled the trigger was dead, as his brother Cario also known as Care managed to get a shot off before he himself died. The Cullen Post newspaper called it the supersized massacre, the double homicide that happened in the McDonalds' parking lot in broad daylight. The waiter walking over to Phifer's table broke him out of his thoughts.

"May I get you anything else, Mr. MacCall?" she asked.

"No, thank you, Pamela," he answered. Taking one more sip of coffee, he rose from the table, buttoned his suit jacket, and left a 20 dollar tip for the waitress.

It was no secret that Phifer did not look like the monster he truly was capable of being. Nor did he act like it. Although he is a trained killer, he believed in treating people with respect. He had not done a murder for hire job in eight years, and vowed not to go back to the life. Until now. This would be the grand finale. Phifer is an architect with a love for fine structures and quality property. Being as good as he is at his job, he made a completely lavish life for himself, donating to countless charities and foundations. His logic is to allow the good to balance out with all the bad he's done. But there was this woman, Grace London, his final subject. A cold look formed in his eyes that sent chills down the spine of those watching. "Time to pay the piper," he said as he exited the restaurant.

Grace

"To Grace London. We could not have anticipated the type of asset you'd be to this business. We would like to thank you and humbly ask if you will accept said terms as a token of our appreciation. So as the young people say, to the bag!!" The vice president of Modern Realty lifted his glass to toast.

"To the bag!" everyone said in unison and laughter.

"Now Grace, do not drink too much, you still have that meeting with the client in ten minutes," the VP said half jokingly.

"Absolutely, sir. I'm heading to the conference room to prepare the brief. Thank you everyone!"

Grace said as she headed down the hall. This day meant a lot to Grace. Not only was the President of the realty firm giving her the capital for new projects to be sold under her very own London Realty, but he had arranged for Grace to meet the contact in person to discuss the property design. Grace stood at the huge round table, preparing the documents, and there was a tap at the door.

"Hello, I am looking for Grace London," said the most handsome man Grace had ever seen. She cleared her throat. "I am Grace London. Is there something I can help you with Mr.…."

"MacCall. I'm sorry. My name is Phifer MacCall. I am here to discuss specifics on an upcoming architectural project," Phifer said reaching out his hand.

"It's great to meet you. Please, have a seat. I wasn't expecting you just yet, but we can begin now," Grace said. There was something about MacCall, Grace couldn't pinpoint it. One thing she did know was that Mr. MacCall was fine as wine. Milk chocolate, tall, with just enough muscle frame to peek out through the suit he wore. "This will be interesting," she mumbled as she walked over to the monitor to begin her presentation…

Grace

It had been almost a month since Phifer and Grace had begun their project. Things were going great. Phifer had been everything Grace's boss said he would be. They had spent a lot of time together, late nights, and a few times meeting over dinner. He had been a complete gentleman. Grace hadn't spent this much time with a man since her late boyfriend Cario. This particular night, they were working late again. Wrapping it up, Phifer asked if he could take her home, seeing as he had a car pick her up that afternoon.

"Sure, why not?" she said. As she gathered her belongings, she noticed Phifer looking at her. Not checking her out, but more so with a puzzled stare.

"Why are you single?" he blurted out. He was just as surprised as her.

Taken aback by the question, she hesitated. "I guess it's God's plan, for now." She couldn't help but notice his eyes. On the surface, they were cold, but underneath that, she saw a man that she had begun to like…a lot.

She grabbed her Kate Spade jacket and walked out the door with him in tow. The car ride was silent except the smooth jazz playing on the radio of his BMW. Grace wanted to invite Phifer in for a glass of Chardonnay, but a small voice inside her warned her not to. She figured it was nervous jitters considering she hadn't been on the dating scene in years. "Would you like to come in for a glass of wine, Phifer?" Grace asked looking over at him.

"Sure, why not?" Phifer answered flatly.

"Great," Grace said with butterflies in her stomach. They pulled up to the condo.

"I need to make a call. I will be right in," Phifer assured her.

"Take your time," she said as she headed to the house. Unarming the alarm as she walked through the door, she came straight out of her shoes. She dropped her work bag on her bedroom floor and heard her cell ringing from inside the bag. She fumbled to find it. Finally locating the phone, she answered, "Hi Mema."

"Hey baby, what's up? I haven't heard from you since earlier," Mema said, sounding concerned.

"Aw, I'm sorry. I've been super busy with this project of mine. But we are practically done with everything; we signed all of the contracts today. But I have to go. I will call you in the morning so we can meet to have breakfast. My treat," Grace said.

"Okay, I love you, Gracie."

"I love you too, Mema." Grace hung up and headed to the kitchen to get the wine glasses and Chardonnay ready. With Phifer taking longer than expected, Grace decided to take a quick shower.

Phifer MacCall

Phifer sat in his car, replaying his brother Care's death over and over in his mind. The rage he felt was indescribable, but the feeling he got knowing that everyone responsible would be dead in less than an hour gave him peace. Phifer wouldn't deny that had he been a weak nigga, he would have fallen for Grace. She was smart, ambitious, and beautiful. There were times that he questioned whether she was even capable of conspiring with that kid who pulled the trigger. But he couldn't hear the story without all signs leading to her setting him up.

He sent the text to June: *Change of plans, I will be unwrapping the gift instead. Be at the party in 45minutes to clean up.* Not waiting for a response, Phifer grabbed his silencer, Baretta, and other supplies. Death had become an art to Phifer MacCall, and Grace was about to be his masterpiece. He put everything into his work bag and headed to the house. He disconnected the alarm system and planted a device that prevented cell phone service. He knocked on the door and heard Grace's voice say, "Come on in."

Mema

Something just did not sit right in Mema's spirit. It hadn't been for the last month or so. Her intuition told her to pray. She went to her closet that she called her war room. This is where she prayed and spent time with God. She placed a pillow down, got on her knees and prayed like never before…

Grace

"I don't know why you brought your work bag in here," Grace joked. "The productive part of my brain is out for the night." Grace laughed.

Phifer chuckled and said "touché."

She passed him a glass and he gave her a once over. This time, it looked like he was checking her out. She wore an oversized Nike T-shirt, black tights, and furry slippers. She had her hair doobie wrapped with Bobby pins and her toes were immaculate. They laughed, joked, and listened to music. Grace knew she had overdone it; she was beyond tipsy. She slid off the couch onto the floor and buried her head in her hands. She didn't even notice Phifer planting the gun behind the couch after screwing on the silencer. He sat down next to her, ready to make his move.

With her head still in her hands she said, "He killed him."

Phifer stopped in his tracks. "What did you say?" Phifer questioned.

"You asked me why I am single. I'm single because he killed him!" she said and began to cry uncontrollably. "His name was Cario, but his nickname was Care. He was the love of my life. It was all my fault!! I just had to have McDonalds fries!" she said wiping the tears and snot from her face. "I saw a friend from Psych class, Aaron. We talked for a minute, but he left. Next thing I know, I got my food, and turned around to see Aaron shooting Nate!!!" She wept, deep, hard, and most importantly, she wept sincerely.

Phifer

Phifer was stunned as he sat there and watched Grace cry her heart out. In his days of killing countless subjects he had become a scholar at reading body language and seeing through lies. Using his expertise, he saw not one ounce of deceit nor dishonesty from Grace. *She did not do it, she's innocent. I can't, and I won't kill her,* Phifer thought to himself. His mind wanted to grab the gun, but it was *Heart Over Matter* at this point. He carried her drunken body to her bedroom with his emotions all over the place. The strongest feeling, he felt above all, was relief. "I'll be right back, Grace. Stay here," Phifer said as he walked out of the room. He headed outside to deactivate the machine and put his bag back in the car. He grabbed his cell and texted June: *Abort mission. Explain later.* He put his iPhone back into his pocket and walked back into the house. He lay next to Grace on top of her bedspread and held her tight. It was such a relief to him that he didn't have to feel overwhelming guilt about the person responsible for his brother's death still breathing, or guilt that his heart allowed him to fall in love with Grace. He did still feel some guilt though.

The guilt of having fallen in love with his late brother Care's girl. He kissed her forehead, holding her tight. Phifer watched Grace sleep, thinking: ***As we lay, heart has taken precedent over matter. As we lay, I hold a previous enemy in my arms, yet my heart is spewing love. As we lay, without my brother, without a Care. Without my brother and without her lost love…unbeknownst to her, our hearts mourn the same person.***

Mema

After Mema ended her prayers, she got up with a weight lifted from her chest. She had faith God had worked out whatever evil plan the devil had brewing. It was at that moment, that Mema was reminded how important prayer was and how privileged she was to be a believer. Prayer really does change things.

A Forbidden Love

By

Dalya B. Johnson

Dalya B. Johnson

Dalya Johnson was born in Newark, New Jersey, but currently makes her home in Fountain Hill, Pennsylvania with her amazing husband and awesome kids. She owns and operates several independent businesses. Dalya is a travel agent, a Scentsy representative, and the owner and operator of her own wash and fold business, as well as an online purse boutique. Writing is her passion and outlet from her very busy lifestyle. She hopes you enjoy reading her creative thoughts. If you wish to contact Dalya, she can be reached via email at dalyajohnson@yahoo.com.

Dedication

This passage is dedicated to all the women out there enslaved by the words "I love you." Don't settle for being disrespected just because you're comfortable and don't want to start over. Love isn't disrespectful or hurtful so if you constantly find yourself in that situation, please be strong and smart enough to walk away.

A Forbidden Love

As Kim and Patrick looked into each other's eyes, he could see all the hurt and pain she'd been through and all he wanted to do was heal her from it, kiss it and make it go away like a child's "boo-boo." With each kiss they shared he just couldn't understand why she wasn't being cherished like the queen she was, however, he vowed to make that his job going forward.

Kim was by far the sexiest woman he'd ever laid his eyes on. She had her own career, own crib; hell, her own everything! Why this loser couldn't do his job was beyond him, but he swore a long time ago if he ever got a chance with her, he would be her last.

As things grew intense, he gently pushed her against the wall and began to kiss her neck softly. He knew she liked it from the faint moans he heard and the quivering of her body. He slid his hands down her pants and started rubbing her love-box; by her reaction, he could tell she hadn't felt that in quite some time. She was so moist and ready at that point, with what seemed to be one motion, Patrick slid down her pants, lifted her up in the air and was face deep between her legs.

The pleasure Kim was experiencing was better than she'd ever known with ole what's his name! She really appreciated his attention to detail; as she was on her second orgasm and it had only been a few minutes, but a lifetime in her mind.

Her eyes rolled around in her head as she continued to scream out in pleasure and slob heavily! Patrick finally stopped the verbal assault on her love-box and even though they both wanted to go to the next level they both decided it was better to stop while they were a HEAD! Lol.

Kim could barely get herself together. Her eyes were crossed so much she now needed glasses, that's how great it was. She was looking at Patrick like he just killed her cat or something; in a sense he did. Patrick asked why she was looking at him like that, but she couldn't even get her mouth to form any type of sentence that made sense.

Finally, she managed to utter, "I don't usually do things like this; you know I'm married and all..."

Patrick interrupted Kim; as far as he was concerned, she didn't have to explain herself to him or nobody else for that matter! "Do what you need to do to get your mind right, baby. I'm here when you get yourself together." Tears began to fall from Kim's eyes. "That's the reason I didn't want to take it all the way," he said. "I know you're going through some emotions right now. To be honest, I just wanted to make you feel good." He wiped her tears away, helped her fix her clothes and walked her to her car. Once outside, they shared the most intimate kiss either of them had ever experienced. Sparks flew.

For her, Patrick was a way to keep distracted from the pain she was really feeling, not knowing Patrick would be the best thing that ever happened to her.

Kim started going to the gym more and more because she knew Patrick would be there. Still ashamed of how they met, she couldn't really bring herself to allow him to take her on a real date. She was so worried about what people would say that knew the history between them.

Patrick, on the other hand, could care less and was just patiently waiting for a chance to take her out for real. Patrick knew he could love her past her pain if given the chance. He understood she was scared and wounded so he decided he would just wait and give her time to come around. Each time they were together, he didn't want her to leave. He would literally give her the keys to move into his house immediately, that's how open he was; he had been for years and now that he had a real shot, he most certainly wasn't going to allow anyone to mess that up.

From The Beginning

Kim awoke yet again to an empty bed. The only difference today was that it was their fifteenth-year anniversary. So tired of Byron's bullshit and excuses. As she started packing his bags yet again, she promised it would be the last time (THIS TIME, SMDH). She heard the twins in the kitchen. Wanting to save face for them, but she could never hide anything from them, her face always told on her. The Twins were old enough to understand what was going on; quite frankly they needed this lesson.

She walked into the kitchen. The twins, Taneisha and Kaneisha, Kim and Byron's seventeen-year-old daughters both said in unison, "Hey Mama. Happy Anniversaryyyyyyyy," while they cooking breakfast. The oldest, Taneisha, turned towards her mother and automatically knew something was wrong. "What did the bastard do this time?" she snapped.

Just as Kim was about to answer, Junior, Kim and Byron's sixteen-year-old son, came running into the kitchen. "SMDH. His ass didn't come home last night AGAIN," he said. "Ma, why do you put up with this foolery? You can clearly get any man you want. Why are you just settling for this poor excuse for a man and letting him walk all over you? We're your children, we love you; we'll always have your back, we're tired of seeing you crying and heartbroken all the time."

Kim was moved to tears by what her son was saying. Looking at the girls' faces, she could see they agreed and felt the same way. As a parent you never want your grief to overrun onto your children; in this case she could see everyone had been affected by Byron's actions and was sick and tired of the disrespect.

Kim reassured her children that she was more than fine, and effective immediately, their father would no longer be residing in their home, for the reasons stated obviously. It's no secret that Byron had many women all over the city: they've called her, contacted her on Facebook, one even came to the house looking for him, thinking he lived with his aunt as Byron told her. She got into verbal and even a few physical altercations with a few. Each time he had a lame excuse and after some lying, crying and bomb ass sex, he was forgiven. Not this time!

The one thing Kim could say about Byron was that they had some amazing sex, which got him out of the doghouse most of the time, but she swore this time it was not going down like that. She didn't want to see no tears or hear no sob stories. It was over for good. There comes a time in a woman's life when enough has got to be enough, and Kim was at that point. She was tired of being enslaved to a loveless marriage. She made up her mind the day she woke up to an empty bed on her anniversary, there's nothing he could ever say that would be able to fix this.

Bryon

Byron woke up to 29 missed calls and 17 messages. "Somebody is pissed, I see," he thought. "I'm so tired of playing around with her, but don't want her to go just yet. Gotta make sure I get as much money from her as I can before this thing blows all the way up! She got that little fatty on her and some crazy mouth action going for her, but I'm tired of her attitude and boring ass routine. The only reason I stayed this long is because she got that banging job at the law firm and she made the blueprints on our home come to life. Don't know how I would've gotten that house built without good ole' money bags, I mean Kim, my wife. So, for now I need to try to play nice I guess." He rolled his eyes.

Darlene

"So tired of hearing that damn phone going off all night! Some women are so dumb. If you have to call him all night or he doesn't even bother to come home most nights, then clearly he's not into you and you should just move on. So tired of playing this game with these two, so either he decides who he wants to be with, or he won't have to because I'll walk. She can't handle him anyway, always making him upset and stressed. She needs to just get out of the way and let me get that. This is where he wanna be anyway! Besides, my son is tired of not seeing his dad all the time cause of this bird."

Kim

"Let me call my little sister. I haven't talked to her in a while. I know she's probably in the middle of midterms, but I need to talk to someone, and I know she will listen without judgement," she thought, rolling over and dialing her number.

Kim: Hey boo, how's it going?

Her sister: Hey, love, everything's good. And you?

Kim: Can't complain, I guess. Just waking up, just discovered this retarded dude didn't come home again last night. Today's our freaking anniversary and I started it all alone and I'm so tired of the fuckery!

Her sister: Aww, I'm sorry, hun. Happy anniversary and I'm sorry it started off like this. Are you sure he isn't hurt or something like that?

Kim: That fucker ain't hurt, but he will be when I catch up with him.

Her sister: Lol, you so damn crazy! You wouldn't know what to do with yourself if something happened to that creep. Tired of that asshole walking all over you and treating you like shit. You deserve much better and could get it if his bum ass wasn't in the picture!

Kim: Girl, I'm trying to rid my heart of his silly ass. This is the last straw. I'm over it and over him.

Her sister: UMMM HMM that's what your ass say til he get a hold of that box, then you all in love again. Lmao, so we'll see.

Kim: Shut up. Lol. Don't make me laugh and he ain't even going to get close enough to the box to get a smell of it, let alone touch it! But no, all jokes aside, I'm really done this time.

Her sister: Well, sis, if that's the truth then I'm happy for you. Glad you finally know your worth!

Kim: How's school coming along and my beautiful nephew? I need to get up there to see ya'll, but you know I hate Atlanta's airport, it's absolutely the worst.

Her sister: Everything's fine. My truck is in the shop so I'm having a hard time getting around, but other than that things are going well. Just finishing midterms. Think I'm pulling mostly A's & B's, and your terrible nephew is doing great. Yes, you need to get up here and see us!

Kim: OMG, why didn't you tell me about the truck? I will send you money later today. Is two grand enough to cover it? And I will be up as soon as this case I'm working on is over. Should be in a week or two. I miss you guys, plus I need a vacation from everything and everybody!

Her sister: I didn't want to bother you, and yes, that would help. It's about 1500 to get out and with the rest I will get some food for the house and things for the baby.

Kim: No worries, you should've said something. I know how them damn foreign trucks are. Rovers look good on rims until they on a flatbed, lol. I'll send 2500 so you can get the things you need for you and the baby since that no-good baby daddy ain't around! Don't know why we have such bad luck with men when we're such great women. Love you sis, see you guys soon.

She hung up the phone, smiling.

"Talking to baby sis always puts me in a good mood. Think I will go up next weekend. I need a getaway and some fun in the sun, plus I can spend some time with my new nephew. He's already three months old and I've only seen him once. Let me make an appointment to get this crazy hair braided. Gonna hit the gym later to see if I can tone a little before then so I can kill'em in my bathing suit and tight shorts, plus Patrick's sexy ass will be there."

Just as Kim was backing out of the driveway, Byron was pulling up, both dreading this meeting. Bryon had flowers, a card, and some lame excuse of course. In the past, that would have been enough to get right back on her good side, but not this time. Enough is enough and she decided to continue out the driveway like she didn't even see him, leaving him standing there stuck on stupid.

He also wanted to know where she was going, looking all good. She had on workout clothes, but her hair was done, makeup on point, and she had on that Versace! When he turned to go in the house, he noticed some of his clothes and shoes in the garbage cans in the front; when he got in the house it was no better! "This is one of the reasons I'm leaving her goofy ass in the first place," he thought to himself!

The look on the kids' faces said a lot to him and honestly, he was just over it all. Yes, he still loved his wife and family, but he was just bored being with one woman. He knew he didn't want to be tied down from the beginning, but he didn't have anywhere to go when they first started going on.

Situations turn into situationships/relationships. "Not saying it wasn't good, we've had some great times, but that ship has sailed and I'm just on to better things. When she comes back, I'm just going to have to let her know how I feel. How she takes it, is just how she takes it," he thought.

Byron saw her LV duffle bag on the floor with a few bathing suits and short ass shorts in it! Wondering where the hell she thought she was going, he started looking further into the bag to see a few thongs, etc. Mouth open and instant attitude, he says out loud, "This heffa is cheating on me!" He immediately began calling Kim's phone. "Now this bitch doesn't want to pick up!!!!!!!!!!!!!!!!!!!!!!"

(Ya'll see where this is going, right??!!!! Make sure you read "HIS MAIN SIDE CHICK" coming out late July 2019.)

AS WE LAY WITHOUT A CARE

Rising From Defeat

By

Heidi Mercado

Heidi Mercado

Heidi Mercado is an ordained Reverend, Minister, Evangelist, and Pastor. Both she and her husband are the Pastors of House of Freedom Worship Center. Heidi Mercado is a Preacher, Teacher of the Word of God, Empowerment Speaker, Co-Founder of Soul Searching Ministries, Inc., a Chaplain with the United Chaplains State of Pennsylvania, a Credentialed Domestic Violence National Advocate,

CEO of R.I.S.E, a wife, a mother of five and a grandmother of two. Heidi Mercado has an Associate's Degree in Paralegal Studies from Bronx Community College, a Bachelor's Degree in Criminology from John Jay College of Criminal Justice and a Master of Arts in Christian Ministry and Discipleship at Liberty University. She is currently a Doctorate student at Liberty University with a focus on Christian Education. She is also an Independent Consultant for Paparazzi Jewelry. She is the owner of Sparkling Touch, a cleaning business, and she and her husband are the directors of the United Chaplains in Pennsylvania where they both teach chaplaincy classes. Her passion is to preach the Gospel of Jesus Christ with the message of FREEDOM, that those in bondage may be set Free by the power of the Holy Spirit.

Rising from Defeat

"Oh no, the police are here!" These were the words I said numerous times as a child when I was growing up. For some reason there was always chaos in my home. I'll never forget the day the phone rang: It was the hospital; they called to notify my mother that my brother was in a coma. My heart was beating so fast. I remember watching her almost die at the news. I don't know how she managed, but she told me to quickly get dressed to go to the hospital. It was not long before my brother came out of the coma, probably hours, that we had a sigh of relief. The fact that I have a God-fearing, prayer warrior kind of mom, the prayers were heard. God answers. I knew from this moment. God is listening, I knew. God is real and he's watching.

Every time the phone would ring at my house, it was almost always something going on that involved going to the hospital, police station or the court. I watched my mom time and time again have a look on her face as if her world was ending. I wondered how she was still managing to keep it together when everything around us seemed to be falling apart.

But I watched how she kept striving; she continued to do whatever she needed to do to maintain normality in the house. For the years to follow, I witnessed the strength of my mom. She was not easily broken and when she did break down, she always got back up. I must say, I learned to persevere by watching how she stood amidst the tests in her life and I learned from a very early age, that survival would be my response mechanism.

AS WE LAY WITHOUT A CARE

I had many hopes and dreams. I had a big dream. Of course, as a child I didn't know how I would accomplish everything I knew God placed in me, but I would certainly find out. While I was still in High School, I became pregnant with my daughter; this was the beginning of an entirely new course for me. I was in for a rude awakening. All the dreams I had would now come to an end, or at least I thought. But there was something inside of me that still desired to do everything I could to reach my goals. I knew I had to be an example to my daughter and teach her how to go after her dreams no matter what it would cost. After giving birth, I took care of my daughter and did all the mommy things. After about a year or two, I managed to go back to school. I did not have anyone to care for my daughter, so I enrolled her into the daycare at the campus I attended. To my relief, my school offered students the opportunity to enroll their children in daycare while attending classes. This was a blessing for me. I was able to earn an Associate's in Paralegal studies. I was so happy! I knew I was working towards my future. I remember thinking that I could do anything I set my mind to. So, I ran with that thought.

After earning my Associate's, I wanted to earn a Bachelor of Arts from John Jay College of Criminal Justice. I prayed to be able to get into that school, and by God's grace I was accepted in and now I was on another course in my life. I remember always wanting to be a lawyer. As a child I would pretend I was a lawyer and I would argue my case before the judge. I was convinced as a child I would win the case for my client. My passion has always been to advocate, to defend the cause of the voiceless. It was never about fame or popularity, but everything to do with justice and a fair trial. There was this burning fire inside of me that I simply could not extinguish. Every fiber of my body cringed at the witness of injustice. My mind was settled. I knew this was the path for me.

I majored in Criminology because I wanted to get into the mind of a criminal. "Why do criminals do what they do?" "What is the force behind their decisions?" My logic was: "If I can only figure out what is in the mind of the criminal then I can help them." I was excited to be learning what the profile of a criminal was and the details of a crime scene. I was blown away by the teachings and the hours of reading case after case. I was on target, a girl on a mission! I knew where I was going, and I was going to get there. I knew because I knew I wanted to become a Criminal Defense Attorney. And no one was going to stop me!

While on this journey, this bus ride that I call it, many things took place. People got on the bus that should not have been with me. There were times I was supposed to get off the bus and I didn't. And yet, there were times I did not belong on that bus in the first place. But it was where I was at; it was my ride, my journey, so I rode it. And as with every turning point in life, I was faced with decisions to make. I was now in the real world with real issues in front of me. I was in a relationship that was very toxic, very unhealthy, and because I became used to living in disorder, when I met my disorder it seemed normal, it seemed it was part of my journey. I lost myself. I cannot remember the exact moment it happened, but I lost my identity, and I was a young woman with many questions and no answers.

It would be a long time before I found myself. And while being in what I referred to as "my wilderness" I never lost hope. All the thoughts of my childhood and not having my father present in my life played a big part in my perspective on life. Off and on, these thoughts would surface at unexpected times. As I look back, I realized I was in bondage. There were strongholds that I had neither the knowledge nor the power to come against it.

I yearned for clarity, for answers, for guidance, but instead I was more lost and lost in a world that I felt was drowning me in and I could not escape. It was during these years, as a young mom trying to make ends meet, working, going to school and doing everything possible to get out of the mindset I was in. But it did not matter where I worked or what degree I was pursuing, I was in a jail in my mind. I was plagued with thoughts of an absent father and I could not let it go. I questioned God many times and asked him, "Why did I have to be the child that grew up without a dad?" I was not saved when I would ask God these questions, but for some weird reason I believed he always answered me by saying, "I have something planned for you." This was the hope that kept me going for years.

I did not know what would happen or how it would happen, but I knew this much: "There's got to be more!" I was in a mess for ten years of my life, living a life that became known to me as a cycle of repetition. I kept doing the same thing and hoping for a different result. I lived as if there were no consequences, living as though I had all the time in the world, living as though someone would rescue me out of the pit I was in. But when you have lost your identity, when you are lost and you can't find your way home, you keep going hoping you will get to where you need to be.

Some years went by, and by this point, I was tired of being tired. I felt as if I was not going backwards, but I was certainly not going forward. One day I remember so clearly, my friend Dolly called me on the phone and said to me, "I'm picking you up, you need to hear from God." I told her, "Don't bother, I don't want to go to church." She insisted and even picked me up. She appeared at my house and said let's go! So, I got dressed, got the kids dressed and went to church. That day, while the preacher was preaching, I was sitting at the back of the church, and he called me to go forward to the front. I was so nervous, I was trembling because although I was not saved, I've always had the fear of the Lord and I was like, "Oh boy, this man is going to reveal something." Well he did! This man told me everything I was going through, I mean everything. And he told me what I needed to do.

I remember going home so happy because I felt God had heard my prayer. I went home. I felt empowered, but within a few weeks I felt that I was living a life with no purpose and a repetitive cycle of bondage again. See the problem was this: I received a word from God, and I thought, "Well now, God will move the mountains for me and everything will be fine," but that's not what happened. Because as you may know, God won't always move your mountain, but he will be with you as you climb it. I realized much later in life, God does not remove situations. He gives you the tools you need and then tells you to work it. God spoke to me and said, "Where you walk, I will be with you, but you must stand knowing who you are and whose you are." I felt like, wow! God is trusting me to stand; okay then I need to stand and know that the God that I profess is the God that will never leave me and will lead me.

Something had to give, and what I didn't realize then that I realize now, is that I had to give up everything he was telling me to give up. This was difficult for me. I had to trust God and that was not easy. But I stepped out in faith. With much prayer I was able to finally come out of the wilderness I was in. I took control of the bus ride; in fact, God told me he would lead me if I followed. Oh, I followed. For the first time in my life, I knew God like I had never known him. I had a relationship with him. I knew his language. I learned how to trust him. My faith was increasing daily. I began to love the woman I saw in the mirror; because He loved me first, I was able to love myself.

And though it was challenging at times, it was His voice, God's voice that I heard, and I followed. God said to me, "Fear not, for the enemies you see before you, you will see no more!" (Exodus 14:13) Wow!!! How amazing was that! I can truly say, he staged everything for me, he gave me strength I didn't have, he gave me confidence I didn't have, he gave me my identity and he told me who I was. He reminded me of the spoken word over my life and he told me if I will just follow him, my life will never be the same.

Thankfully, after so many years of having a lost identity, years of drama, years of pain and fear, years of crying myself to sleep and beyond all of that all the years of bondage, I was finally free! That was the day I woke up and I realized how beautiful, how awesome God made me. That was the day I realized he "fearfully and wonderfully made me." (Psalm 139:14) That was the day he reminded that I was His and I could walk fearlessly. I'll never forget that day because it was the day I felt His power pour into me. I looked at my past and everything attached to it and I said, "No more! You cannot control me anymore; I know who I am, and I know who I belong to!" I know all hell was trembling. I had decided. I decided to be free from everything the enemy had me under.

I didn't get my years back, oh, but he gave me so much more. He gave me a second chance at life. He placed an awesome man of God in my life who was and is my shining armor. He blessed me with five amazing children and two beautiful granddaughters. I felt like the princess who was kept in a locked room waiting for her prince to come. Well my prince did come, and he came with a sword to rescue me! This was the time in my life where I felt like, oh my God, I can breathe again. I really felt like I was holding my breath for years and I finally had my breakthrough.

I didn't become a lawyer, but God afforded me the opportunity to advocate for women who have been abused. I have an organization called R.I.S.E which stands for Restored, Inspired & Standing Empowered. I fight for justice and I stand in the gap for women who have said "no more." The courtroom where I bring my cases is the courtroom of heaven. I bring women to the feet of Jesus so they too can experience freedom and a second chance at life.

I had to trust God's process for me. His plans are so much better than mine. And now, I look back and I don't regret anything. That was my story; it's not my whole story, but it's part of my story and without that story I would not be where I am today. By the grace of God, I have overcome, I have been restored, I have been inspired and I am standing empowered. My mission is to let women know who have been broken that there is hope, that God has not forgotten them, that no matter what they had to face, there is still a light that is shining so bright for them.

I rose from defeat and even better, I rose and looked at my adversary and said, "God has me! God took my ashes and gave me beauty; he took my chaos and made it my testimony; he took my mess and gave me a new start. Every crooked area in my life, he straightens it. When I decided to trust God with everything, He restored me and gave me a new life in him.

The Other Side of Karma

By

Charlotte Marshall Murray

Charlotte Marshall Murray

Charlotte Marshall Murray has been writing since the age of eight years old. She began at an early age telling stories to her parents and grandparents, thus beginning her love for storytelling. Charlotte loved to write poems and plays for her church during the holiday season. As she got older, her love for writing continued to grow and she was accepted to The Philadelphia High School for the Creative and Performing Arts where she majored in creative writing. After high school, she attended Grambling State University for two years, majoring in Journalism. Ultimately, she graduated from Lincoln University of PA, where she earned her Bachelor of Arts degree in English. In February of 2018, Charlotte earned her Master of Arts Degree in English/Creative Writing from Southern New Hampshire University.

Charlotte Marshall Murray is the author of six books. They are *Broken Hearted, Same Ol Song, Broken Hearted II Secrets Revealed, When the Heart Turns Cold 1, 2, 3*, and *Black Ice The Family Bloodline* which is the latest book in the *Lady Ice* series. Charlotte has published with Nayberry Publications and Imperial Publishing, both headed by Shani Greene Dowdell. She is also a contributing writer in the anthology, *Savor: The Longest Night* with her short story titled *Soul Deep*. In conjunction with her books and short stories, she is a contributing writer for The Urban Release Magazine. She also writes her own column titled "Journey of a 1,000" which showcases the stories of African Americans, both past and present.

Charlotte Marshall Murray is also the founder of the R.O.S.E.B.U.D.S. Mentoring Program where she services young girls between the ages of 7-18. R.O.S.E.B.U.D.S. which is the acronym for Realizing Our Strength and Excellence By Understanding our Destined Success is a mentoring program that addresses issues such as self-esteem, bullying, health and nutrition, college awareness, healthy relationships, and many other topics that young girls face. The program has been in existence since 2000.

Currently, Charlotte Marshall Murray is working on re-releasing her first novel, *Broken Hearted*. In conjunction with that project, she is also working on a vampire series titled *Blood Rites: Year of the Queen*.

She resides in Philadelphia, Pa. with her husband and three children.

Email- jns911@gmail.com.

Facebook page - Author Charlotte Marshall Murray

The Other Side of Karma

Camille awoke that morning feeling refreshed and renewed. She had learned over the years that toxic people wear many hats. They can be your mother, father, family, friend or co-worker. However, Camille never thought in a million years her husband would be that toxic person. Her middle school sweetheart, father of her four children, and co-partner of their family business, The Wright Mark. Camille was on her own, seeking divorce and looking to start her life over. At first it all seemed like a nightmare, but that nightmare became a reality when her husband of 25 years walked out the door. Camille was crushed. She asked herself, "What did I do?" "Why was he not attracted to me anymore?" "Was our sex life boring?" and "Did he feel I was not supportive?" She had no clue. But what she did learn was that it didn't matter how much a woman loved her husband and catered to him. If he wanted to leave, he would. As she sat at the breakfast table, listening to the coffee drip into the pot, she thought to herself, "How did I get here?" How was it possible that she was no longer going to share a home, her bed, and life with her husband? Camille shook her head and mouthed, "Tracy Coleman."

***

Life was as good as it gets for Camille and Broderick. Their children were doing well, and their business was flourishing. The Wright Mark was their editing and publishing company. There were six authors signed to the publishing company and Tracy was one of them. Camille could remember the day she initially met her for her consultation. At first, Camille didn't want to stereotype her, but at first glance she looked like a big butt ratchet hoochie. Her look exemplified the characters she wrote about. But Tracy was nothing like she looked. She was a kind, educated business woman who just liked wearing revealing, tight, form-fitting clothes. Tracy was one of their top selling authors. If she wasn't doing a book signing, she was doing a radio interview or book tour. Her personality was huge, and she owned any room she walked into. Camille could see why her husband became attracted to her. What man wouldn't? Camille later learned that the sweet persona Tracy exuded was just a wolf in sheep's clothing.

***

Camille and Broderick were planning to go on a date later that evening. Their weekly date night had turned into a monthly date night or whenever they could fit it in. The two hadn't spent quality time together for a while. So, it was a big surprise when Broderick told her to meet him at La'Shay's Restaurant. Distance between the two had become the norm, so Camille was hoping to repair that tonight over dinner. She prayed they could reignite the flame.

Camille dressed in her favorite black strapless dress that her husband loved. Every time she wore it, there wasn't much happening but a trip to the bedroom. She was excited and nervous as she drove to meet him. As usual, he had been gone by the time she awoke in the morning and this would be her first time seeing him for the day. She felt like a school girl going to the prom. When she arrived, she entered the restaurant and looked around. She could see him seated at a table drinking a beer. Camille smiled, fixed her dress, and walked over to him.

"Hey," she said.

"Hey," he responded getting up and helping with her chair.

No kiss. No remark regarding the dress. No nothing. Camille began to feel butterflies in her stomach, and she felt something was wrong. She'd known her husband since middle school, so she knew something wasn't right. Just like she knew for that past month, he'd been distant. A million thoughts ran through her mind as she waited for him to speak.

"Um, do you want something to drink?" he asked.

"Yes, red wine, please," she nervously responded.

Broderick gestured for the waiter and ordered her a red wine and another beer for him. He seemed to be nervous and somewhat cocky. As much as Camille wanted to be there with the hope of fixing whatever was plaguing their marriage, she needed to know, honestly, what was wrong.

"Are you ready to order?" asked the waiter as he set their drinks down.

"No, not yet," Camille quickly answered before Broderick could.

"Okay. Let me know when you're ready," he said, walking away.

Camille could sense Broderick's anxiety as he gulped down the beer in a few swallows. The nervous grin he smiled when he felt like a cat who ate the canary filled his face. Camille knew something was going to be said to her that she wouldn't like, so she braced herself for whatever words he would speak.

"Whatever you need to tell me, just say it. We've been together too long for you not to be able to."

"You're right. Okay Camille, I'm moving out. I'm leaving you……"

Everything after the words "I'm leaving you" were spoken, was a blur. Camille felt as if she had been hit by a speeding train. She didn't see it coming. Yes, she knew they had grown distant, but never did she think it had come to that. Moving out, leaving? How did she not see it? Camille looked at him as his mouth moved with words spilling out, but she was not hearing anything. She was numb.

"….. so, I think it's for the best. You can have the house, and as far as the company, you can buy me out. I already started my own publishing company. Camille, are you listening? Do you hear me?"

"Uh, yes, I hear you. So, you're moving out? You're leaving me? Why? When did it get that bad?"

"Listen, I don't want to say it was you or me, but I changed. I need some things that you can't give me. I don't want to hurt your feelings, but we just are not there anymore. You had to know by now."

"What I knew was that we weren't as connected as we used to be. What I knew was that you were distant. But what I didn't know was that it was this bad," she said with tears welling in her eyes.

"I'm sorry, Camille. The last thing I wanted to do was hurt you, but I couldn't lie to myself anymore. Or to you. I'm not happy."

"The only thing that could make a man leave his wife this suddenly and coldly is another woman. Who is she?"

Broderick looked like a deer in headlights. He was hoping he wouldn't have to go there, but he should have known his wife. Broderick hoped he could just say he was leaving and that would be it.

"Who said…"

"Why start lying now? You're on a roll. Who is she?" Camille asked with tears running down her face.

"It's not that…."

"Who is she?" she yelled as she slammed her fist on the table.

The people in the restaurant turned around, startled, and looked at them. Camille could feel her body overheating from anger as her legs shook uncontrollably. She didn't know the man sitting across from her.

"Tracy," he said sternly.

"Tracy? Our Tracy?"

"Yes."

"So, all the late-night meetings, early Saturday outings, new client consultations were just bullshit excuses to meet her?"

"No, I mean, not every time. Listen…."

"Listen to what? You said it all," she said, standing up and grabbing her clutch bag. What you can do for me is come get all of your belongings and get the hell out of my house."

Camille turned to walk away as the waiter returned with a confused look. Broderick shook his head and chuckled while ordering another beer. With a full moon and sky filled with stars, Camille walked out of the restaurant feeling as if her world had come to an end.

***

Five months had passed, and things were moving slowly for Camille. She got up every day, washed, dressed, went into her home office to work, but she felt like she was just existing, only going through the motions. Tracy Coleman had left the company to follow Broderick, so Camille was working harder to ensure the rest of her writers had the same success. Her children had come over every day after her husband left, but the frequency of their visits was starting to dwindle. Camille knew she had to let them get back to their lives so she could get back to hers. Each day got easier, but she still had a long road to travel. One of the hardest things was seeing Broderick and Tracy in public and at certain events. She always remained a lady, but she wanted nothing more than to see them both hurt the way she did. One thing that kept her going was knowing: What goes around comes around, and sometimes what you lay down with, you don't get up with.

**

It was the Christmas season and Camille was in a much better space. She had started counseling and it was really helping her to get her life back on track. She was learning to laugh again and love herself more. Camille had vowed to never make a man the center of her world, ever again. Being single had put her in a different market, but she wasn't ready to date again. Although she and Broderick were going through a divorce, she was still married, and she still honored her vows.

Camille was flabbergasted when she received a phone call from Broderick asking if he could stop by later that evening. She hadn't spoken to him in months, and after she got over the initial pain he caused, she was fine. Camille didn't want to reopen any wounds that she had healed and covered. However, her curiosity got the best of her. She couldn't for the life of her figure out what he wanted, but she would find out that evening.

***

AS WE LAY WITHOUT A CARE

Broderick arrived at her house at 7:30 pm. He was supposed to be there by 6:00, but he phoned to say he was running late because he hadn't been feeling well. When Camille opened the door, she tried not to allow her expression to convey what she was thinking. He didn't look well at all to her.

"Come in," she said as he walked into the house. Camille closed the door and headed toward the living room. Broderick followed behind. He sat on one chair while she sat across from him on another. She couldn't pinpoint what was wrong with him, but it was something. He looked tired and a little smaller than he was the last time she saw him.

"Do you want something to drink?"

"No, I'm fine. You look good, Camille."

"Thank you. So, you wanted to talk to me?"

"Yeah. Uh, it's been some time since we saw each other or even talked to one another. A lot has happened with me since then."

"Oh yeah? Like what?"

"Well, for starters, Tracy and I are no longer together."

"Hmmph. Sorry to hear that."

"Oh no, it's cool. Man, I was so wrong – about a lot of things."

"So, what is it that you're trying to say, Broderick?"

"I'm sorry. I am so sorry that I left you and gave up on our marriage. I'm sorry for hurting you. I'm sorry for you having to see Tracy and I out together. I know it had to hurt."

"It did. For a long time, but God, therapy, and red wine got me through. I'm okay." She smiled.

Camille could sense that Broderick had more to say. She didn't know if she should pry or just let it be. However, he had come this far so he may as well tell her everything.

"Is there something else you need to tell me?"

Broderick took a deep breath and looked at her. There was extreme pain and regret in his eyes. Camille almost felt sorry for him, but she didn't. Although she had forgiven, she would never forget.

"I love you Camille. I never stopped. I…."

"What's wrong?"

"I want to come home. I never should have left. I was wrong."

"You want to come home? Why? Why now? It's not because you love me so much. What is going on?"

"Okay, Camille, okay. I'm sick."

"Sick? What do you mean *sick*?"

"I don't know. They've been running tests for the last month and they still don't know what is going on with me."

"What are your symptoms?"

"I've been losing weight as I'm sure you see. Cramps in my legs when I walk. Just a lot of things going on."

Camille wasn't sure how to take the news. She didn't know whether to jump up, run to him and hold him, or to just say nothing. No matter what they were going through, she still loved him, and he was her husband. But she had finally gotten to a space where she could say his name and not break down. She was learning to be alone, but not lonely. She was learning to accept that she was responsible for herself and no one else. The biggest lesson she learned was that her husband walking away had nothing to do with her. It was him.

"So, why do you all of a sudden want to come home? Where is Tracy? I mean, I know you said you two broke up, but she does know you're sick, right?"

"Let's just say that when the shit hit the fan, she ran."

"So now you think it's okay to come back to me? What do you want me to do?"

"Camille, I know I messed up, but I was hoping you could at least consider reconciling. Listen, I don't know what's wrong with me. Hell, I could be dying. If that's the case, I want to be home, with my wife and my kids."

"Forgive me if I seem callous, but you should have thought about that a year ago when you invited me to dinner to tell me you were leaving. Listen, I pray all goes well but I can't go backwards. I'm in a good space and that's where I'm staying."

"You don't even want to think about it? I know you still love me. I still love you."

"I do love you, Broderick, but I'm not in love with you. I wish you well, but we are through. That's it. Nothing else to say."

"Baby," he said, getting up and walking over to her. He reached down and took her hand to pull her up.

Broderick hugged her around the shoulders and looked down at her. Camille still found him to be the handsomest man she had ever laid eyes on, but there was no "them" anymore. He destroyed that. He destroyed the trust, commitment, loyalty and love they had for one another when he laid down with another woman. She couldn't go back, for her peace of mind and sanity. Camille stepped away and smiled.

"If you had asked me to come home about five months ago, I would have helped you get your clothes and unpack. But you didn't, and now we're here. I will pray for your health. I will pray for your life. But that's all I can do. I wish you well, Broderick."

Camille walked to the front door and opened it. Broderick hesitated before following her. She stood to the side as he walked out. He turned to face her with remorse and regret in his eyes.

"Well, what can I say? I made my bed, so I have to lie in it. Just know that I love you and if you ever want to try again, call me," he said with a trembling voice.

    Camille smiled as he reached down and kissed her on the cheek. He walked away, with Camille feeling an array of emotions. One thing she did know was that she was strong and in control of her life. Camille was reminded of a quote that said, "Don't look back. You're not going that way." That was the new story of her life. She was moving forward, and life was looking grand.

A Chosen Life

By

Yvonne Hernández

Yvonne Hernández

Actress and playwright, Yvonne Hernández, is best known for her monologues and short plays. Her play, "Queer Monologues and Short Plays," has been performed at The Alchemical Acting Studio in New York City.

In her "One Woman Show," she tells stories of some of the most interesting and fascinating people she has met in her life. A nosey next door neighbor, a young man killed in his prime for simply being gay, and many more. Her stories are chock full of quirky characters that will make you laugh and cry the night away. Her piece in this anthology, "A Chosen Life," deals with the dark side of child abuse and how it can send the human soul spiraling into a frenzy of uncontrollable behavior.

A CHOSEN LIFE

A One Woman Monologue for Stage Performance

A woman slowly walks onto the stage. She's wearing hospital pajamas and slippers. She looks about. There is obviously something mentally unstable about her. Something frightening about her. She starts to speak.

Chosen. I was simply...chosen. Chosen to live the life that put me exactly where I am at this very moment. Here, in this cold room adorned with a metal-framed bed and bars for curtains. People always made cruel remarks about the cake baking moms of the 50s, but I so envied them. I wanted what they had. I never asked for this. I was put here by a power much higher than me and I've had to pay with the rest of my life.

I was bad before I was even born. Did you know that? So I was punished by being born to people who did not love me, who hated me, who resented me. My mother couldn't even look at me. My father, on one of his inebriated nights, beat the hell out of her. He broke her collarbone then raped her, broken bone and all. My mother got pregnant with me that night. You see now? I was a curse when I was conceived.

My mother couldn't stand to look at me. I don't blame her at all. You see, I was this awful thing that happened to her and because of it...she could never kiss me. I never felt the warmth of her breast because she could never hold me to tell me that she loved me because...she didn't. I could still see the contempt in her eyes; I could still feel the hatred resonating from her soul. I made her the way she was because I was born bad.

I also did bad things which angered my father. He would try to sleep late on Saturdays, but I woke him as I played with my doll. My Nancy Nurse doll. Well, I had to be punished because on top of being bad, I was ungrateful. My father worked hard so that we could have nice things, and I thanked him by not listening, by not letting him sleep.

My whole life, doctors have told me that what he did was not punishment. That punishment is one thing and cruelty is another. If you ask me, the doctors are the ones who belong in here. What do they know? They weren't there when I woke him from a sound sleep....

(*She suddenly looks around, quietly. It is obvious that there is something mentally unstable about this woman.*)

I was just a little thing playing with my favorite doll, Nancy Nurse. I disturbed his sleep. He got up, wrapped my long, beautiful hair in his fist, and dragged my tiny body for what seemed like an eternity. I was only six years old. After he stripped me bare, he poured water all over me and then proceeded to whip me with that thick, leather belt. I remember the belt had studs on it. He used the water so that the strikes would sting. My hands were tied behind my back. My mouth was gagged so my screams wouldn't be heard. I had to kneel on two metal cheese graters. Then he put me into the closet for my punishment.

(*She walks about. Eerie. Remembering.*)

Before he closed the door, he made me watch as he took the knife from the dish rack and plunged it into my Nancy Nurse. He cut out her eyes, then stabbed her over and over till there were only pieces of her left. He threw the pieces of my Nancy Nurse into the closet with me and he closed the door. He said, "Maybe next time you'll think twice before you wake me with that stupid doll." Santa Clause gave me that doll, and he had no right to do that. I loved her, and he had no right to do that to her. I don't remember how long I was in there when he finally opened the door to let me out, but I do remember how the light coming in from the window hurt my eyes. How the cheese graters and dried blood were stuck to my knees. He yanked the graters off my knees, like pulling off a Band-Aid, quickly, so it wouldn't hurt. I think that was very considerate of him, don't you? I mean, to pull the Band-Aid off quickly so it wouldn't hurt. Then he poured rubbing alcohol all over my body. I can still feel how it stung, how it stung.

(She rubs her body as if re-living the experience, then suddenly stops.)

Don't look at me like that! He had to do it. He did it because, in his own way, he loved me. He poured the alcohol into my wounds to prevent infection. I think that was very considerate of him, so stop looking at me like that! All parents clean their children's boo-boos because they love them. Don't you see? The love my parents had for me was different because I was chosen, born to be bad. You see? Oh, never mind. What do you know?

(She comes back to reality and speaks normally again, but almost like a child.)

I was just a teenager when I met Wanda. It was the first day of school. She held her books tightly against her breasts. I remember how I envied those books. How I wanted to be those books. You should have seen her long, beautiful, black, silky hair waving in the breeze. What a sight. My heart skipped a beat. She caught me staring at her and I didn't care. I'm glad she saw me. She smiled and came over to me. She said, "Hi. I remember you. We were in the same 5th grade class together. You sat in the last seat, in the last row of the class."

I suddenly felt embarrassed. I was sure she remembered how I never paid attention and how I failed every test. Mr. Cullen, my teacher, always laughed when he handed back my paper with the big red "F" on it. I was very quiet. Always stared out the window and never paid attention. Mr. Cullen always humiliated me by telling me, in front of the whole class, that there was something obviously wrong with me, and the whole class laughed at me. Except for one cute little girl who sat in the second seat in the second row. Wanda. She never laughed at me. Then, one day came when I just couldn't take it anymore. Mr. Cullen handed back my test with yet another big red "F" on it and he laughed, again. As he turned to walk away he mumbled something. He thought I didn't hear him but I did. He said, "What difference does it make? She's a lost cause anyway."

That angered me and I yelled out, "Go to hell, you jerk off! I hate you! I hope you die."

He turned and looked at me with the same contempt I often saw in my mother's eyes and the hatred of my father's wrath. He said, "What did you say to me, you little shit?" Then he grabbed me so hard by the shoulder that he tore my dress. He dragged me to the closet where the kids hung our coats. It was one of those closets with the sliding doors and rows of hooks.

(She starts to cry, an angry cry.)

He tried to force me in there. To close me in there. I couldn't let him do it. Suddenly, I felt this power come over me that I had never felt before. I grabbed a pencil from Anthony Lamato's desk. He had just sharpened it at the metal pencil sharpener at the window, and I plunged it into Mr. Cullen's arm again and again. The final plunge broke off the tip of the pencil into the palm of his hand as he tried to defend himself, but I kept stabbing at him. I couldn't stop. Something came over me. A hysteria. And I just couldn't stop. He tried to grab me but he couldn't. *(Angry)* I wouldn't let him. He ran out of the class like a punk ass chicken shit and I felt big, empowered. I was Superman and Wonder Woman all rolled into one, and the entire class was frozen and bug-eyed as they looked at me. They weren't laughing at me now. They looked at me with fear, with respect, and I decided right there, at that exact moment, that not allowing anyone to turn me into a mealy mouse was a power I can possess if I really wanted it – and I *really* wanted it.

I got a taste of power. It became a drug injected straight into my veins and I was addicted instantly. It gave me life. It became the air I breathed. Suddenly I didn't hate Mr. Cullen anymore. I appreciated him for bringing out this power that I had in me all along. A power I never knew I had. That was the first time I was sent away.

Funny, I had forgotten all about that, but the memories came back when Wanda mentioned the fifth grade. Then I thought, why should I be embarrassed? I stood, proud. Knowing surely that she must have remembered me as the hero who stabbed the shit out of Mr. Cullen.

Then she said, "Don't you remember me? I sat in the second seat in the second row."

I said, "I remember you. You always wore a pony-tail with a bow to match your dress and you were the skinniest kid in the class."

She laughed and I told her that I was sorry, that I was not making fun of her. That I thought she was the cutest kid in the class and, wow, how beautiful she still was. She thanked me and said, "Well, look at you. You are so pretty." She said I was pretty! I suddenly felt awkward. My face flushed. My knees nearly buckled and I felt butterflies in my stomach. My head and my feet felt warm. I felt dizzy, wonderfully dizzy.

We got to know each other, Wanda and me. She didn't like that I played hooky. She thought it was sad that I still got bad grades. I had to pass by her house to get to school. I made sure to pick her up every day and for the first time in my life, the colors of autumn looked so vivid. Winter felt wonderfully cool, spring was deliciously breezy with the fresh scent of flowers, and the summer... as warm as a newborn baby.

I started to go to school and I liked it. For the first time, I liked it. My favorite class was English Literature. I loved to write. It was my sanctuary. She loved the stories I wrote. She took it upon herself to show a story I wrote to one of the teachers and he loved it. He said it was very good and that he couldn't believe that such a young woman could write with such depth. He showed my writings to other teachers and they agreed. They had to come to my class to meet this talented young girl. Me! They said I had...a gift. A gift! Me!

Wanda helped me with my homework and I helped her with anything she needed to write. She gave me life. For the first time, I knew how it felt to live, to love, to be joyful of life. My grades improved. I mean, they were amazing. Wanda talked to me about scholarships. She told me that if I applied myself I could get one. She pushed me to apply myself and I did. I wanted that scholarship.

AS WE LAY WITHOUT A CARE

I was always at Wanda's house. I loved being there. Her parents appreciated their good fortune. Their born-good child. I could feel love in Wanda's home and it felt wonderful. She came to my house...once. I could see it in her eyes and I could feel it from her soul that she could sense the coldness in my house. My father eventually told her, "Go home, girl. Or don't you have a home?" My mother, as usual, cowered in her room. She never even came out to meet Wanda. Wanda never came to my house again. I didn't want her to.

I was at Wanda's house one Saturday afternoon. Her parents went out. We lay in her bed reading, when she took the book from me and she kissed me. She said we should practice kissing so that, one day, when we got ourselves a boyfriend, we would know what to do. I thought, "I don't want a boyfriend," but I didn't particularly feel like discussing it at that particular moment. We kissed and I suggested, while we're at it we should practice petting, and she agreed. Her breasts felt wonderful, like water balloons filled with warm water and they tasted like strawberry ice cream, only better. Her insides felt creamy and tasted so sweet. Like the cake batter I dipped my fingers into as a child. My stomach felt weak and I felt a warm flow come out of me and onto my panties. Then I told her, "I don't want anyone but you." She said she felt the same but she didn't know how to tell me. She cried and said that we must be weird girls and I told her, "No!!" That she should never feel that way. We cried, we laughed, and for the first time in my life, I was loved and I could give love, and this new feeling scared me and thrilled me.

Time slipped away from me. It got late and I hurried home. Afraid because I knew what awaited me, but I didn't care because the thrill of Wanda's aroma engulfed me. I got home. That's when my happiness came to an end.

(She cries a feeling-sorry-for-herself cry.)

I was born bad, so happiness was something my fate was not going to allow me to have. I walked into the house. By this time my reflexes were amazing. I knew my father was behind the door. I ducked quickly. He missed striking me with that god damned belt and I was able to grab it in midair. That enraged him. He screamed, "I'll kill you if you don't let go." I knew at that moment that he meant it. I knew at that moment...it was him or me. I felt that power come over me again and I knew if someone was going to die tonight, it was not going to be me.

Then he said it. Something I was just not going to allow. He said, "You were with that little whore Wanda, weren't you? Well, I'll fix her wagon if she ever comes here again."

I suddenly remembered my Nancy Nurse. I couldn't allow him to do that to Wanda. To someone I love so much. I had to stop him. I looked at the dish rack and I saw a sharp pencil. Like the one on Anthony Lamato's desk. Only, it wasn't a sharp pencil. It was the chef knife. The same one he butchered my Nancy Nurse with. I plunged the knife into my father's arm, severing veins. The second stab plunged into his carotid artery. The third severed his lungs in half and the final one perforated his heart. He died instantly. D.O.A., the hospital said.

(She laughs.) I found love and lost hate all in one night. I felt euphoric as I sat in the police interrogation room. Just like Norman Bates, as his mom at the end of the movie *Psycho*, I didn't say a word. I just thought of how I was going to see Wanda as soon as I got out of there, but they didn't let me out.

I heard Wanda was horrified when she found out what happened. She never came to see me. I never saw her again. Her parents wouldn't allow it. I loved her and I love her still. I will never forget her.

I finally got out, but through the years, I got into a lot more trouble because people are cruel and they make me so angry! So, getting rid of them, eliminating them from this world was what I just had to do. Well, here I am. In this room with this metal bed and those metal curtains.

ENTER: Audrey, a full-figured nurse. Through the years, Dolores has grown fond of and loves Nurse Audrey like the mother she never had.

AUDREY: Dolores, honey, who are you talking to now?

DOLORES: I'm talking to them.

AUDREY: Oh, them. You mean your audience?

DOLORES: Yes, my audience. Don't you see them?

AUDREY: Oh yes, I see them.

DOLORES: Actually, I'm getting more material to put into my book. My memoir.

AUDREY: Honey, you are a good writer and your story should be heard. Dr. Joe says he will help you get it published, but sitting here talking to yourself won't get it done.

DOLORES: I'm not talking to myself, Miss Audrey. I'm talking to my audience. Don't you see them?

AUDREY: Yes, I forgot. *(Looks out.)* Nice looking audience. What an imagination you have, Dolores honey.

DOLORES: They are not my imagination. If you look hard, you can see them. They really are there. My story will be a book, then a play. If you behave yourself, I may include you in it. I think lots of people will all come to hear my story. Don't you?

AUDREY: Yes, baby, I do. Now come on. It's time for your lunch.

DOLORES: *(Hugs Audrey and buries her face in Audrey's chest.)* Do you think Wanda will come to hear my story? So she can understand that I am not a horrible person?

AUDREY: Yes, baby, I do. Now come on.

DOLORES: I love your boobies. Do you know I love boobies? There's something so motherly about them.

AUDREY: Yes, I know. Now come on. Time for lunch.

DOLORES: Wanda has nice breasts. They taste like strawberry ice cream. Did I ever tell you that?

AUDREY: Yes baby, you did, about a hundred times. Now come on.

DOLORES: My mommy never hugged me, but I think she must have had nice ones too. Do you think she must have?

AUDREY: Yes, I'm sure she did. Now come on. Time for lunch.

DOLORES: I know. You said that already, silly lady. I love you, Miss Audrey. Wanda, you, and Dr. Joe are the only people in this world who have ever been kind to me.

AUDREY: I love you too, Dolores honey. Now come on. *(She helps Dolores to her feet.)*

The two women walk off stage, talking while Audrey has her arm around Dolores, patting her on the shoulder.

SCENE, LIGHTS OUT

AS WE LAY WITHOUT A CARE

My Husband, Her Ex

By
Rashonda Jones Aiken

Rashonda Jones Aiken

Rashonda is a mother and wife. Being raised by her single mother and grandparents, along with aunts, great grand-aunts and a slew of older cousins, she was taught to be independent, humble, open-minded, and generous and was told to always respect her elders. Rashonda was the only child for ten years until her younger brother came along.

While Rashonda was taking care of everyone else, she had to make sure she got time to herself. She started reading different books here and there. Not any specific genre, but something to read to herself.

A few years later, Rashonda joined a book club in New Jersey named Black Voices. The book club dispersed, and everyone went their separate ways. Rashonda kept reading various authors' books, but she had a few favorites that she would follow.

About ten years ago, Rashonda found another book club, but at that time, no new members were being accepted. A couple of months later, Rashonda attended a meeting for the book club to see how they operated. She liked the book club and knew a couple of the members from her hometown. Rashonda was accepted into the book club, named Literary Ladies Book Club out of New Jersey. Rashonda is currently a member for the past nine years. She is also L2 Facebook and Twitter administrator for her book club.

Rashonda is the CEO and a children's book author under her publishing company Rahway Girlz

Publishing, along with her daughters Se'Quince and Wynter. Se'Quince is an author with four books under her name. Wynter is the web designer for Rahway Girlz Publishing. Wynter is currently working on her first novel and a poetry book while studying Journalism and Communications in college as a junior at Kean University.

Rashonda was born and raised in New Jersey and lives there with her twin daughters, husband, and cat Brownie.

(Instagram) @rjonesaiken

https://www.facebook.com/AuthorRashondaJonesAiken/

My Husband, Her Ex

Alexis was on her way to the convenience store to buy some groceries when her cell phone started buzzing in her back pocket. It was Benjamin texting her. She ignored the text while driving. She was only two minutes away from Kroger's. She just needed to get a few items to prepare dinner tonight. She wanted to make a special dinner for Benjamin and herself to talk about their marriage. It hadn't been that great for awhile, so she wanted to do something nice by candlelight. She grabbed what she needed, and as she was leaving the store, her cell phone started buzzing again. It was another text message. She ignored it again and started putting the groceries in the car. Now her phone was ringing. It was Benjamin calling.

"Hello!" she answered. "What is it, Benjamin?"

"What took you so long to answer my call, huh?"

"I was buying stuff from the store. Sorry! Anyway, why the sudden call?"

"I have to make appointments to call you to answer me?" He was being sarcastic.

"I will be home in twenty minutes," she replied, and then hung up the phone.

Upon arriving home, Alexis parked in the front of the house since it was closer to the kitchen. She got out and walked up to the door to open it. Bella, their maid, greeted her to help with the few bags she had. Bella was going to help Alexis prepare dinner tonight. She told Bella if she stayed a little past her time, she could come in late tomorrow. She was okay with that. As they put the stuff away in the fridge and cabinets, Alexis started walking towards the front of the house, calling Benjamin. He didn't answer. She called him again and no answer. *Well how convenient is that; he can blow up my phone, but he is not even answering me,* she thought. She called out one more time. He yelled from the den that he had turned into his office space. As Alexis walked in, Benjamin just started bickering at her.

"All this long time, I cannot believe my mother was right about you," Benjamin yelled across the room.

"What are you talking about, Benjamin?" Alexis started to cry, trying to figure out what her husband was talking about. He was starting to scare her a little bit. She was a very emotional person, so when anyone started yelling or accusing her of something, she got very upset and started crying.

"Shut up your crying and get out."

"Wait a minute. Get out for what?"

Benjamin was fuming with so much anger and was turning red in the cheeks. But what else was a man supposed to do when he found out that his wife cheated on him with another man? His best friend, no less, so he thought.

"Did you really marry me for my money?" Benjamin released a pained laugh. "I thought you were different than the other women I dated."

"I am different than all the other women you fooled around with. I don't ask much from you, Benjamin, but to be loyal to our marriage, me."

He asked the question again. "Did you marry me for my money?"

"Benjamin, what are you talking about? Of course not. I did not marry you for your money. I did not cheat on you. I would never do that. I love you!"

"Are you cheating on me with someone, Alexis?"

"No, I have not cheated on you, Benjamin. With anyone. Why are you asking me that?"

"You cheated on me with my best friend," he accused.

"I didn't cheat with anyone, especially not Larry," she said, shocked.

"I filed for divorce, Lexi," he said. His tone was dry, like he was done talking. Dismissing her like a little kid.

Lexi didn't like to hear those words, "divorce." She always knew her life and her marriage weren't always rosy, but she never thought it would come to an end like this. She thought this was excuse for Benjamin because she believed he was the one who was cheating. She wasn't sure with whom, but she could feel it in her gut. He was just using her to get his way so he didn't get caught.

Before accusing Alexis of an extramarital affair, Benjamin must have met with his personal attorney, Lucas Grant, prior to him accusing her. He probably told Lucas that she was having an affair and wanted divorce papers written up so he could give them to her. She knew it was a two-week process to file the paperwork through the courts. Once the papers came back, Lucas sent Benjamin the divorce papers. Those must have been the papers that arrived at the doorstep as she was driving up the driveway from the store. She had noticed someone at the front door talking to Benjamin. He quickly closed the door before she could park.

After their heated conversation and accusations, Benjamin gave Alexis a big yellow envelope which contained the divorce papers for her to sign. Benjamin already had her bags packed, hoping she would sign the papers and leave without argument. Alexis read over the papers and started crying.

"You want a divorce that fast over accusations that you only making? You are saying that I had cheated and you know damn well I didn't. You don't want to hear what I have to say about this!"

"No, I don't! This is what I want and that's it."

She signed the papers and threw them at him. She walked out of the den to go pack, but noticed her bags were already packed and waiting. He was walking behind as she was going upstairs to pack some items.

"I had the maid pack your bags," Benjamin said.

Lexi swallowed, fought back her tears, and said, "So, just like that we're over?"

He turned his back. "You should've thought about that before you screwed my friend." He walked away and never looked back.

Alexis stood in silence, until she turned and left the room. Alexis grabbed her bags and left out the front door. She turned and took one last look as she loaded up her stuff in the back of her gray Lexus RX SUV. This would be the last time she would see Benjamin. She wanted no part of him or the memories that came with it after that fiasco. Alexis started her truck and pulled off down the long driveway to the street.

Her heart was just broken into a thousand pieces. What is she going to do now, she thought? She wasn't working anyway. She had put her career on hold after her and Benjamin married years ago. As she was driving, crying, Alexis called her sister Andrea to tell her the news.

Andrea already knew, but she wouldn't tell her that. Andrea was in the house when Benjamin accused her of cheating. She wasn't the one who was cheating.

Andrea's phone kept ringing until it went to voicemail. Alexis hung up crying and kept driving.

The Four Seasons Hotel was within a few minutes drive of where Alexis was, so she pulled into the parking lot. She got out and went inside to get a room for a couple of nights until she figured out her next step. Alexis walked up to the front desk and there stood a tall, thin woman with brunette hair. As Alexis stood in front of the desk, the front desk associate said, "Hello, my name is Melanie, how can I assist you today?" Alexis requested a suite for three nights. She pulled out her American Express credit card to pay for the suite.

"Sorry, madam, it declined," Melanie said.

Alexis said, "Please, try it again." The customer service rep tried, and it declined again.

"Sorry, madam, but do you have another card or cash to pay with?"

Alexis stood there crying. She couldn't believe that Benjamin had already cancelled her credit card. She wiped her tears and said, "I'll be right back." Alexis went out to her SUV to get her tote bag. She had some cash she had been saving for an emergency. This seemed to be the time of an emergency.

She went back inside with the cash to pay for her room. The bellboy helped Alexis with a couple of her bags to her room. She tipped the bellhop whose name was Derrick, from what his name tag said. Derrick unlocked the door for Alexis and they went inside.

    Alexis sat down and started crying again. She couldn't help it, or think what's next. She called her sister again, but no answer. She left a message saying that she was at the Four Seasons on Raritan Road. Alexis got up and went to run some hot water for a nice bubble bath. In the meantime, she called for room service for some wine and food. Because after what just happened, she needed to relax and the wine would do the trick. Her nerves were shot.

    She ordered a bottle of red cabernet wine that is her favorite and a chicken Caesar salad. She wanted something light to eat. For some dessert, she splurged for some chocolate cake to eat later with more wine. While waiting for room service, Alexis grabbed her towel, her scrunchie for her hair, bath and body shower gel, and cell phone, and went into the bathroom. She got undressed and tiptoed into the hot water. She played her playlist from Pandora. She slid down in the water as hot as she could take it and sat down. She blew out a big sigh and closed her eyes. More tears fell.

Alexis cried so much, she drifted off to sleep. Her phone was buzzing but she didn't even hear it. The phone kept buzzing and buzzing until it fell off the side of the tub. Alex jumped up so fast, she forgot she fell asleep. Twenty minutes later, there was a loud knock at the door. She jumped up out of the tub yelling, "Just a minute." She grabbed her robe and wrapped it around her to answer the door. She peeped to see who it was. It was Andrea, her sister. She opened the door and more tears started to fall. Andrea hugged her sister without saying a word. It was quiet for about ten minutes. They sat down and stared at each other.

Andrea said, "What happened?"

She already knew, but wanted to hear Alexis say it. Alexis started out saying that Benjamin accused her of cheating. Andrea's eyes opened wide.

"I never cheated on him, ever. Without giving me a chance, he had already had divorce papers drawn up and ready for me to sign. I had no time to even explain to him that I wouldn't do that," said Alexis.

"I think he's the one that has been cheating, but using me as the excuse. I can't prove it, but what does it matter anyway. I knew we were rocky, but never to the point of getting a divorce."

Andrea just sat there, listening and fumbling around, trying to decide if she should spill the beans that she's the one that Benjamin has been cheating on her with. She was hiding behind the secret doors in the den when the argument broke out. Andrea continued to sit and listen while Alexis kept crying. Andrea got up and went to sit next to Alexis in the chair.

She asked, "What are you going to do now?"

Alexis went on to explain that her credit card was declined when she tried to check in. She had to pay cash instead. Andrea knew that was Benjamin's doing. He was just being mean.

Andrea knew Benjamin all too well. They used to date years ago, but Alexis doesn't know that part of Andrea's history. Andrea is a good, respected lawyer. She works for the law firm Benjamin, Becks and Cooper in downtown Atlanta. She was in the top of her law school class at Harvard Law. She worked hard days and nights to get where she is now. Andrea met Benjamin after she graduated. They met through mutual friends. They were becoming friends with benefits on and off for years. Andrea had broken it off with Benjamin because he wasn't the type to be with just one woman. He had a few in his back pocket, and not just women either. Andrea didn't like it. Benjamin wasn't happy, but he got over it until the next person.

Andrea's career was moving forward in the direction of trying to be partner. She worked the long hours and did what she needed to do, but Benjamin put a damper in her plans. He wanted a booty call one night and Andrea said no. He pleaded with her and she gave the same answer – no.

That was a night that Benjamin was drunk. He had just celebrated opening another club. He wanted to thank Andrea for helping him with the legal paperwork. Andrea knew how he got and wanted no part of it. Benjamin got pissed off and did something dirty. He had some photos of Andrea in some bad and compromising positions that no one should see. He sent the pictures to Thomas Beck, his good buddy from the law firm. He was upset, but intrigued of the moves that Andrea could do. That wasn't a good look, but he wanted in on the fun. Thomas thought he could use the pictures to rope in Andrea; since he knew she was up for partner, he would blackmail her.

The next morning, Thomas called Andrea into his office. Andrea knocked on the door and went inside. She sat down in the brown chair in front of

Thomas' desk. He started the conversation saying how proud he was of her. Everyone had taken notice and he wanted to express his gratitude. Andrea was blushing, saying thank you, until Thomas got up from his desk. He walked around and sat in front of her. Andrea was starting to feel uncomfortable. She pushed the chair back some, with a light smile. Thomas went on to say that he received an e-mail with some disturbing photos and wanted to share.

Andrea had this look like, "What photos, and why are showing them to me?"

Thomas said, "They are photos of you."

Andrea said, "What? What kind of photos do you have of me?"

Thomas got up and walked back around to the other side of his desk to show Andrea the photos. Andrea almost passed out.

Thomas tried to use the photos to get close to Andrea. He had been trying for some time now, but she never gave him the playing card. Well, Thomas thought this was his opportunity. He said, "I won't show anyone these photos if you will have a nightcap with me."

Andrea said no. He asked again. She said no again.

He said, "Well, I guess I must show everyone these photos. The other partners may not like this and that will take away from you trying to be partner."

Andrea said, "Are you blackmailing me for a nightcap?"

He said, "Yes!"

"Well I guess you can show them, because the answer is no. You and the other partners will have my resignation in the morning. Before I leave, who sent the pictures?"

"Benjamin Hamilton. Why?" Thomas said.

"So, I'll know who I am up against," she answered.

Andrea walked out, walked back to her office, grabbed her purse and left for the rest of day. She took the elevator to the parking garage. She grabbed her cell phone to call Benjamin.

He picked up on the first ring like he was waiting for her call. "Hello!"

"Benjamin, where are you?"

"I'm home. Why?"

"We need to talk now." The phone went dead. Andrea started up her black Infinity Q50 with a light tint on the windows. She sped out of the parking garage and headed over to the house where Benjamin and her sister Lexi lived. The drive was about twenty minutes the way Andrea was driving. She pulled up around back, so no one would see her car, especially Lexi. She went into the house from the back and met with Benjamin to discuss the photos. He admitted to what he did, but wasn't sorry. Andrea was furious. The conversation went nowhere.

Ten minutes later, Lexi pulled up with shopping bags. Andrea hid behind the secret doors. Lexi walked in the foyer of the house and unloaded her bags in the kitchen. She called out for Benjamin. He said, "I'm in the den."

Lexi walked in, but noticed tension was in the air. It had so much tension you could cut it with a knife.

All this time, Alexis was listening. That's when the argument started about the cheating. Andrea saw from the look on Alexis' face, that she was all confused. She was blindsided by Benjamin's accusations. Alexis never knew about Andrea and Benjamin until years later. Alexis always assumed that Andrea didn't like Benjamin because they would snip at each other. She thought it was a love/hate brother-in-law relationship.

At the hotel, Andrea told Lexi to gather her stuff up and bring it to her house.

"I cannot do that, Andrea. I don't want to be in the way."

"You won't be in the way of me, Brent and Adam. You can stay in the guest house for privacy or the main house."

Alexis got dressed while Andrea grabbed some bags and took them out to the car. Alexis came out five minutes later and followed Andrea home. Andrea called Brent and told him the news. He was waiting. They both arrived, and Brent came outside. He hugged Lexi, grabbed some stuff and they went inside. They all went and sat down in the kitchen. Brent put on some coffee. Andrea went to go change clothes and came back down. More tears started to fall down Lexi's face. Brent was lost for words. He stayed quiet.

Brent asked what her next step was. Lexi didn't know. It had been awhile since she worked. Her love was cooking. She cooked all the time when Benjamin would have clients for business over to the house. Instead of hiring a chef, she hired herself because she loved to cook. She did all the planning and cooking.

Brent knew someone who was looking for a chef. He offered to talk with his friend. Lexi got excited and said, "Yes, please do so." Brent walked away to make the call. In the meantime, Lexi pulled out her laptop to freshen up her resume real quick to have it ready just in case.

Brent came back and said, "You will be receiving a phone call from someone name Michael Castilino. He owns a restaurant in the downtown area. He's been looking for someone for awhile. The chef he has is not working out the way he wanted it to."

Twenty minutes later, Lexi received the call and an interview was set up for tomorrow morning. She ran and hugged Brent to say thank you. She took her stuff out of her suitcases at the guest house to see what she was going to wear. Andrea was smiling and kissed Brent on the lips to say thank you. Andrea didn't see Lexi for the rest of the evening. Not even for dinner.

The next morning, Lexi drove over to the restaurant for her interview. She met with Michael. They introduced each other. Michael said, "Let's go to the back." The interview was doing a cooking test. Michael said, "I need to fill this spot today before we open. This is what's on the menu."

SICILIAN BRAISED SHORT RIBS

Braised in a Madeira-plum tomato sauce with seasonal spring vegetables and potato puree.

"I need you to prepare this. Everything is in the kitchen. Let's go!"

Alexis was nervous at first. She was talking to herself first to get her thoughts and feelings in order. She kept saying *you can do this*. "Ok, I'm ready!"

Michael left the kitchen and went back to his office. Two hours later, Michael came back to the kitchen sniffing around with his mouth watering, drooling at the lip, with a smile on his face. Lexi had just finished creating the dish with the entrée. Michael took a taste test and was amazed. He said, "You are hired. Can you stay to prepare for the opening tonight at 4:00 p.m.? Lexi said yes. Michael took her for another tour of the restaurant, so she would know where everything is.

Five years later...

"Guess what, Mommy! Look what I made in school today." Austin, my four-year-old said. Austin looks so much like his father; he has his brown eyes and chocolate brown hair and cocoa skin. Oh, did I mention he has Benjamin's cutest dimples too? Yes, he does! Yes, we have a son that Benjamin doesn't know about.

You're saying to yourself: why not? Well, after Benjamin had filed for divorce, I was broken because he assumed I was having an affair. I have never cheated on my husband, but I believe he has cheated on me numerous times. I have no proof, but I had always had this gut feeling. When Benjamin said it was over, I didn't know what to do. I stayed with my sister and her family. She let me stay in her guest house in the back of the main house. Brent helped me get a job working as chef.

After my divorce was final which was about five years ago, I had a complete breakdown. I've managed to go back to work doing what I love to do – cook. I managed to work hard for Austin, even though my sister tried her best to help. I told her not to because I didn't want to continue to feel I was a burden. With Brent's help, I am now the top chef at this amazing Five Star restaurant called "Xen." Michael is awesome. Benjamin felt that I didn't need to work because he had money. His money! Over the years, I saved money for an emergency. My emergency fund went towards raising Austin. The paper that Austin drew in school was a drawing of me and him.

For a four-year-old, Austin has great writing skills that he inherited from my dad. He was a writer. He had three published books about science that were best sellers. I think Austin, one day, will be a great writer and an artist. He's good at making up stories to go with the picture.

I know one day I will have to have that conversation with Austin about his father, Benjamin. I never knew where to begin. But I need to tell Benjamin first, but it seems like Andrea did that for me. She kept telling me I should, but I never went further with the conversation. Benjamin treated me horribly during the divorce. He treated me bad. He wouldn't give me any spousal support. He didn't give me anything. He cut up my American Express credit card. That was my backup when I don't have any money. I consider it my "go-fund-me" card.

"Why did you tell Benjamin about Austin? Andrea!! You are so dead!" Austin overheard me yelling at his aunt Andrea.

"Mommy, when is Daddy coming home?" he asked. "Do my daddy love me? Why did he leave me?" And that was my biggest weakness. I don't like to see my son upset. The way he always says "Daddy" melts my heart and makes me cry. I know I am bad person for keeping him away, but he hurt me so bad, I couldn't do it.

"No Austin…Daddy loves you very much. He's just so busy to visit." Oh, how I hate to lie to my son. During my pregnancy, Austin helped me heal my broken heart by piecing back my heart by loving again. When he was in the womb, I would sing to him while rubbing my tummy. He felt calm. It was soothing to me. I would play soft music. I would lay on my bed without a care in the world except my son. I would stare at the ceiling until I fell asleep.

Beep! Beep! Beep! The sound of the alarm goes off. I lay there for a few minutes. I stoop up, put on my slippers and went to the kitchen to cook breakfast. I went to start on Austin's favorite breakfast, eggs and bacon.

Every morning when I get to up cook, I sit back and think about how everything ended with Benjamin and me. I keep thinking about how this journey all began. I keep going back to my meltdown over the divorce. I started to feel sick off and on. During work, sometimes the smell of the food would make me nauseas. I couldn't stand to be in the kitchen. Michael had noticed a change in my work. I couldn't focus on what I needed to do to prepare meals. My mood had changed. I would snap when I shouldn't. I just felt horrible. Michael sent me home and said to take the night off. Instead, I went to the doctor that afternoon. They drew some blood and did some tests to determine the problem. Two days later, I was called in to see the doctor for the results of the blood work. I was told I was pregnant. I started to cry. I don't know if they were happy tears or sad tears. I left the doctor's office and went home to adjust to the news. I had a lot to think about. What was I going to do?

I never told Benjamin about Austin because I didn't think he would want to be a father to him. He was never around. He was always busy with work. When we were married, I only time I really saw him was when he had people over for business and when I needed to cook. I didn't always get the attention I wanted, but I dealt with it because I loved him. I also thought that I didn't want the fight of asking for money to help raise his son. Every dime I was making at the restaurant, I was saving to get my own place one day. I couldn't live with my sister forever. Andrea and Brent stepped in from time to time to help. I would work long hours to save money to buy our own place. The guest house wasn't big enough for two people. Andrea and Brent put a deposit on a small two-bedroom penthouse with a one and a half bathroom. It was amazing. It wasn't too far from work. It was a new development in the downtown area of Atlanta.

Today at work was going to be busy. Michael had a dinner party this evening at 6:00 p.m. I needed to hurry up, so I could get there to prepare the food, appetizers, go over the wine and whatever he has planned for. After rushing Austin to finish breakfast and to get dressed, we were running behind. I grabbed my purse, keys, Austin and we left. We arrived at daycare five minutes late. Mrs. Williams doesn't like her students to be late. I kissed Austin goodbye and left for the restaurant.

When I got inside, I saw Larry, Michelle and Victor hanging around. Larry is my best gay friend. Well, I met Larry through Benjamin. They were best friends from college years. Benjamin thought I was cheating with Larry on him, but Benjamin didn't know Larry was gay. That was one secret that Larry kept from Benjamin. Larry's lifestyle was kept private because he knew how Benjamin felt about gay people.

When I met Larry, we became very close friends. We were like brother and sister. I never judged him on his preference and lifestyle. I think that is why he trusted me with his secret. We would always hang out and Benjamin didn't like it too much. He was jealous of our friendship that he assumed we were having an affair. We just let him keep thinking it all these years.

As I walked in, who do I see sitting at the back table with two other guys? Benjamin! I tried to hurry towards the back, but it was too late. He saw me. He got up and called my name. I stopped, turned around, and said, "What?" He was stunned, but started to stare. The conversation wasn't flowing so I walked away and went towards the kitchen. Hours later, who do I see again waiting outside? Benjamin. He followed me to my car. As I unlocked my door to hurry to get in, he slammed the door.

"Where you going?"

"Why, Benjamin?" He was getting angry. "I need to leave, so move." I pushed him away, but it did nothing. He asked again. I didn't answer. He grabbed me by my neck and asked again. I said, "D-day c-care c-center."

"Get in my car now." He drove to the daycare center where I said. I got out of the car and waited.

"Mommy, mommy!" Austin said, screaming my name. I smiled and looked towards Benjamin. Austin saw me looking around and he saw Benjamin. "Daddy"! Benjamin looked up at me, confused. Austin looks just like Benjamin. I have a picture of me and Benjamin in my room. Austin knows what he looks like, but never met him before. He started smiling, but had this confused look. I walked towards Benjamin with a frown.

"Is he mine, Alexis? Is he my son? Why did you keep him a secret from me?"

"Why do you care why I kept him a secret?"

"How old is he?"

I looked in the other direction, trying not to make any tears. I wiped them away and turned back and said, "He's five."

"Five! He's five years old and I am just meeting him now!"

"Yes! Unlike you, he has brought joy to my life." I turned to my son. "Austin, I want to introduce someone to you. This is your dad. Benjamin, this is your son, Austin."

"You're just like your sister."

"What does that mean?"

"You two like to keep secrets," he said.

"What's her secret?" I asked.

"She never told you?!"

"Told me what! Just tell me already because I have nothing else to lose."

"You sure about that, Alexis? It may cost you your sister."

"You know what? Forget it. Just take me back to my car. I need to get home."

Benjamin just stood there watching me. In the car, it was very tense to me, but not for Austin. He just kept talking to Benjamin like he knew him since forever. Benjamin asked again why I kept his son away from him.

I said, "I didn't think you wanted him."

"Why would you think that?"

"Because you threw me away."

He looked at me side-eyed with an annoyed look.

"Are you going to tell me the secret that you mentioned before?"

"I don't think you can handle it."

"Why not?"

"Like I said, it will cost you your sister."

"What about my sister? What did she do so bad that it will cost our relationship?"

"She's my ex."

THE END

AS WE LAY WITHOUT A CARE

The Heat of the Sun

By
Kim Carrington

Kim Carrington

Kim Carrington has written novels professionally since 2004 when she joined the BET/Arabesque imprint, which published her first novel, *A Special Place*. Additionally, she has written romantic short stories for *Black Bride & Groom Magazine*. Her fictional short stories have been included in several anthologies.

Kim graduated from the University of North Florida, where she earned a Bachelor's degree in English with a minor in creative writing. Currently, she is employed with Duval County Public Schools. She works at Southside Middle School as an eighth grade English and language arts teacher, and also leads a creative writing class.

Although originally from Pittsburgh, Pennsylvania, Kim has made Florida her home for the past twenty-five years. She lives in Jacksonville with her husband Victor, and two of their children.

The Heat of the Sun

After a long and difficult day of reading briefs and filing motions at the courthouse, Lyz was ready to head home, relax, and enjoy a glass of wine. It was Friday, and although she had a mountain of paperwork to do, she decided that getting in some "me time" was more important.

"Girl, let's get out of here," her law partner and best friend, Kai Jefferies, said as she entered Lyz's office.

"Kai, I told you when you asked me earlier that I wasn't up to going out tonight. I just want to go home and chill."

"Lyz, I'm not trying to get in your business..."

"So don't," Lyz said and started filing.

"But…you did say that Ron wouldn't be home until Sunday night. Let me treat you to a night out. I already got us tickets to a comedy show at Stella's Lounge."

Lyz smiled as she continued filing, knowing that Kai was only trying to help her through a difficult time.

"Asking Ron for this divorce is going to be the most difficult thing I've ever done."

"I understand, and I hate that you're going through this. Promise to call me if you need anything?"

"I promise, and thank you."

Reluctantly, Kai left the office.

I can't believe I'm ending my marriage. It was supposed to last forever, at least that's what we promised each other the day we got married. I can't even put my finger on the exact time things went wrong.

Lyz drove home. When she got there she opened the garage door and saw Ron's car parked inside. She went inside.

"Hey, Babe," he said.

"Hi, I wasn't expecting you until tomorrow night."

"We finished early so I got to come home a day ahead of time. You don't seem happy to see me."

"I'm not happy, Ron, and you're not happy either. I..I think it's time that we call it quits before we grow to hate each other," Lyz stammered.

"Wow, I didn't expect to come home to this. I love you, you know."

"No, I don't," Lyz replied as she wiped her tears away.

"Babe, remember the raffle ticket that we bought from Kai's nephew's high school band fundraiser? We won the cruise to the Bahamas."

Lyz chuckled.

"What's so funny?" he asked.

"Now you want to spend time with me? The last time you really paid me any attention was at Stella's Lounge for our anniversary."

"I want to get our marriage back on track. We owe each other one more try."

They were the words Lyz needed to hear. She looked long and hard at the man she'd promised to love and cherish for the rest of her life.

"I have to think; I can't answer you right now."

Ron slept on the sofa that night, and Saturday morning he awakened to hear Lyz in the kitchen.

"Good morning."

"Good morning, would you like some coffee?" Lyz asked.

"Yes, please."

"I've decided that I want to go on the cruise with you."

"That's great, Babe. When do you want to go?" Ron asked.

"This week."

"I don't think I can clear my schedule off that fast."

"You're the one that said you wanted to give this marriage another try. Show me just how important I am to you right now, Ron."

He contemplated his position as the CEO of WatchTech. He could assign someone to handle things for a week while he was gone, and he did.

A couple of days later, Lyz and Ron were driving down to Miami to take a cruise. During the drive, Lyz found herself laughing at Ron's silly jokes. Once again, she felt like she was the center of his world.

Six hours later, they arrived in Miami, and after parking at a long-term lot, they took a shuttle to the Port of Miami and boarded the *Norwegian Sky*. Their luggage was taken off their hands at curbside, they checked in, and eventually made it to the eleventh floor for lunch and drinks until their cabin was ready.

Lyz was looking out over the water when she suddenly noticed her husband was staring at her.

"What?" she asked as she took a sip of her rum and *Coke*.

"I have questions about this marriage, too, Lyz."

She inhaled deeply, allowed the salt air to linger in her lungs, before letting as much anxiety escape her body as she possibly could as she exhaled. Lyz's eyes met his, and in them she saw something she hadn't seen in a long time, which was his undivided attention.

"What do you want to ask me?" she said.

"Why you decided to just ask me for a divorce and not try to work on our marriage?"

"Ron, you're never home. How are we going to work on our marriage?"

"Lyz. You know that my job requires that I work late and travel a lot. We decided that we wanted to buy the house with big backyard and do a little traveling before we had kids. And what about the kids we planned to have?"

"We can't think about starting a family when with this marriage in such a mess," Lyz replied, tears now flowing down her checks.

"I don't want to see you cry. That's not what this trip is supposed to be about. Let's take a walk around the deck and get some fresh air."

They walked around on the deck in silence, each deep in their own thoughts. Eventually they were allowed to enter their cabin. Ron opened the door and allowed Lyz to enter first.

"Wow, I never imagined that a $5.00 raffle ticket would net us all this," Lyz said.

"I upgraded our cabin."

"You did?"

"Yes, I did. This is the most important trip we've ever taken; our marriage is riding on this one."

It had been a long day and they were both exhausted, but they freshened up and went to see a comedy show at the Stardust Lounge. It was what both of them needed to lighten the mood, and Lyz felt as though she deserved it after not going to Stella's with Kai. The comedian was fantastic and the couple laughed until they were crying. Later at dinner, they shared a bottle of wine and continued to laugh and talk about the show. Eventually, they grew quiet, and the real reason they were alone in the middle of the ocean could not be ignored any longer.

Lyz looked at her husband; his light blue t-shirt stretched across his chest and revealed the muscular six-pack that she loved to touch. His hair, although cut low, was how she liked him to keep it. She reminisced about how she enjoyed being curled up on the sofa at home to watch a movie while she played in his hair. They wouldn't get too far into viewing the movie before they were on the floor, butt naked, and making crazy-mad love.

"What do you think about that?" Ron asked.

"Huh? I'm sorry, I didn't really catch what you said."

"Baby, I was saying that we need to do more of this. We haven't made much time for each other for almost a year trying to get ahead. You at your firm and me at work, it's a plan that's not working for us. I'm willing to give it all up if our careers are going to destroy our marriage."

"I don't want that either," she replied.

"I want you, Lyz," Ron said as he caressed her arm from across the table.

"Ron, I'm feeling what you're saying, but we have to figure out just what we're going to do after the cruise ends."

"I'm not talking sex, although if you're game so am I," he said smiling coyly.

Lyz giggled.

"Seriously though, I didn't mean sex; I meant that I want you to be in my life every day of my life. I want to come home to you, spend the evening and weekends with you, and not at the office, on a plane, or in another city."

"I want that, too, but what are we going to do about that?"

"Remember Max Williams, the head of the IT department at WatchTech?"

"Yes; why?"

"Well, he and I want to open our own business. I can't think of a better time than now. I'll be very busy at first but I can promise I'll be home every night for dinner."

"I like your plan and I think I'll lighten my workload so I can be home early, too," Lyz said smiling.

"He moved over to sit next to her and kissed her cheek. Lyz lovingly touched his cheek and began kissing his lips. The warmth of Ron's body and the scent of his skin made her want her husband more than she could stand.

"Let's make it an early night and head up to our cabin before we get kicked out."

"That sounds like a good idea to me," Ron replied as he stood and helped Lyz out of her seat.

They made their way to their cabin as quickly as they could. They had barely allowed the door to close behind them when they started to undress each other. Lyz undid Ron's zipper, pulled out his manhood, and enjoyed the fullness of him in her hand. Ron's tongue entered her mouth as he unbuttoned her blouse. He didn't bother to remove her long skirt with high slits on either side. He sat on a chair, slid his hand underneath her skirt until he reached her lace panties, and then pulled them off. Next, he raised the skirt over her thighs before he guided her down on top of his hardened member.

Lyz moaned with pleasure as he entered her and then rhythmically and in complete harmony their bodies made love to each other. Ron held Lyz's hips snuggly as he grinded hard and purposefully inside her. Then his fingertips went everywhere he knew she liked: her thighs, belly, and nipples.

He's not playing fair. He knows he's not playing fair. I love this man more than I love my next breath, and I...I...

Lyz lost her thoughts in a frenzy of passion. Her body trembled in passionate shivers, and her breathing got faster until she cried out in lust for him. Spent, she leaned onto Ron's chest, but he wasn't finished with her yet. Still hard and inside her, he picked Lyz up and carried her to the bed. He laid her down, and with a free hand he knocked the rolled towel elephant off the bed.

Now, he took Lyz to the heights of pleasure they used to enjoy before their busy lives got in the way. His lips teased and pleased the nape of her neck before devouring one nipple and then the other. Each soft brown tip begged for more attention. His finger and thumb would massage the tips of her breasts while his mouth was busy loving the other.

Ron stopped briefly and rolled Lyz onto her belly. He knelt between her legs and then pulled her hips up to meet him; he entered her again. Lyz moaned and enjoyed her husband taking her from behind. She came again, and after Ron knew she was well pleasured, he allowed himself to delight in the depths of her wetness. His thrusts were now deeper and more intense. He pounded inside her with a need and fierceness that made him moan until he filled her with his essence. Finally, exhausted, the couple collapsed and fell asleep without a care.

When Lyz awoke, Ron had showered and was dressed for the day. He had on a simple white t-shirt and a pair of swim trunks.

"Good morning, sleepy head," he said as he kissed her on the lips. "I made plans for us to go snorkeling. We have to get out of here and join our group."

"What time is it?"

"8:00 am."

"Ron, it's so early. After last night I thought we'd sleep in, order room service, and just take it easy today."

"Oh no, Ms. Johnson, we're here to work on the whole marriage, not just our sex life. Now come on," he said giving Lyz a playful smack on her rump. "We are going to have an amazing day. I'm going to give you something to think about if you want to try to walk out of my life." He kissed her again and left the room. After he had left, Lyz took a quick shower, dressed and went to meet Ron for their excursion on the island of Freeport.

They left the ship, and after a short bus ride it was another twenty-minute ride on the boat, before they reached the most beautiful blue/green waters. While they sailed, they enjoyed hamburgers and *Cokes*. The boat also had a slide that dropped off into the water. Lyz slipped out of her cover-up to reveal a sexy little black two-piece swimsuit with gold accents. Ron's eyes weren't the only ones glued to Lyz's beautiful body. She pulled her hair band off of her wrist and pulled her hair up in an afro-puff. As she did, another man watched admiringly.

"Hey bro, do you mind?" Ron asked with an attitude as he moved to block the guy's view of his wife.

Lyz chuckled, grabbed Ron's hand, and led him away saying, "Come on, Baby."

Lyz couldn't help but think of how Ron had acted when another man simply looked at her. Although she didn't see him, she imagined he was looking at her a little too long to suit Ron. She had to admit to herself that, although it was not her intent, she did love Ron's reaction.

They enjoyed seeing all the amazing fish and the reef, and when they were tired they swam back to the boat and relaxed. The boat had made its way back to the dock, and the couple decided to walk around Freeport for a while. It was incredibly hot, and Lyz was fanning herself. Ron bought her a bottle of cold water, and the couple decided to walk to a nearby secluded beach. Once there, they found a little pavilion where they sat down to relax.

"What are you thinking about?" he asked.

"Us, Ron. Right now I feel really close to you, and I want it to continue."

"I know it will continue. Lyz, we want the same things, but we're going about getting them in the wrong way. I see that now. I need to be home with you and you want me, don't you?"

"Ron, I need you, too."

"Then let's do this; let's make each other our top priority."

"I'd like that," Lyz said as she continued to fan herself.

"Okay, and let me tell you one more thing, sexy Ms. Johnson." He brushed the collar of her beach cover-up aside to reveal her swimsuit strap. "You look really good in black."

"Oh, I do," she replied as she took Ron by the hand and led him underneath a nearby tree. She took off her cover-up and spread it out on the sand, and then she lay on top of it and pulled Ron down, too. And there they made love again, in the heat of the sun.

AS WE LAY WITHOUT A CARE

A Gift From Love

By
Sonya Felice Jenkins

Sonya Felice Jenkins

Sonya Felice Jenkins, former model, former professional singer/songwriter, professional and corporate certified trainer, life coach, mentor, entrepreneur, host of the Internet radio show, *"Raven's Closet Talk Show,"* and now a published author.

Stepping from out of the spotlight, now going behind the scenes is where she feels the most comfortable. Writing took hold of Sonya in high school and refused to let go, but the creativity and imagination has always been a big part of who she is and how she had been able to adapt and thrive in various industries over her personal and professional life.

Sonya graduated with an Associates' Degree from Essex County College where she made the Dean's list twice before graduating. She is single. Owner of Life's Puzzle Pieces, LLC and Reaching Prosperity Management. A serious lover of various music/movies/books and various television shows, interests in various hobbies and lives in Northern New Jersey.

Author of the following books: *Once In A Lifetime Love* and *Once In A Lifetime Love 2: The Feeling Never Goes Away*. *Once In A Lifetime Love 3: The Good, The Bad And The Ugly Side Of Love {coming soon}*. Contributing author in *We Rise Above: The Teen Anthology, Rebuilding Your Life Going Forward Anthology, My Soul In The Wind A Compilation Of Poetry {coming soon}*, and other blogs/newsletters.

Contact via email:

authorsonyafjenkins@gmail.com

Social media:

Twitter: @authorsonyafj

Instagram: @authorsonyafjenkins

Website:

https://sonyafjenkins.wixsite.com/authorsonyajenkins

A Gift From Love

There's a strange kind of vibe in the air today. Not sure how to explain it, but there is definitely something different about today, especially at this moment of this mid-afternoon. Gazing out the window, the sun is shining brightly through the unexpected rain shower. The warmth of the sun mixed with the raindrops hits the people on the street like a childhood friend playing a game of tag and everybody is it until they step inside a building or get into their cars.

There are also people walking in the warm rain as if it doesn't faze them; they aren't letting the rain stop them from enjoying their respective day. Looking out her office window at the flurry of activities on the street, the glow of the sun and the water droplets randomly covers her view with the litany of rainbow colors swirling around. Faint colors of orange, yellow, blue and hints of purple hits the glass walls and slowly twirls across the marble floor of her office as the water beads slowly slides down the window.

Her mind and energy level begins to reduce towards a calming state. Moments like this one give her a greater appreciation for the simple things in life. They say in life, life is not the amount of breaths we take, but it's the moments that take our breaths away, which is probably true; however, she also thinks that certain breath-taking moments in life are predestined for us to experience, like being, falling, and having love in our lives. Pure, unconditional, no-holds-barred and over the moon and back, until death, kinda of love is what she appreciates, plain and simple.

She and her husband, Tegene, are a couple who, for the most part, are just your everyday, ordinary couple who enjoys all those breathtaking moments in life. They love each other beyond measure; as stated in the Bible, *"...love never gives up. Love cares more for*

AS WE LAY WITHOUT A CARE

others than for self... Isn't always me first... Doesn't keep score of the sins of others... Always looks for the best, never looks back, but keeps going to the end. Love never dies..." (1 Corinthians 13:8 MSG)

Sure, it may seem strange to quote the Bible, however, she did say there was a strange vibe in the air, but nonetheless, she and Tegene do have a love bond that is ultra-strong like Gorilla glue and Flex Shield mixed together; nothing would dare try to break it. No matter what is going on around them, she and Tegene can sense within them if the other isn't happy, not feeling well, upset, angry or in danger somehow.

Their relationship core foundation consists of friendship, truthfulness, loyalty and making each other happy above all else. "Who could ask for more than that?" she thought as a solemn smile grew across her face as her cell phone rings.

"Hi!"

"Hi, yourself, handsome."

"How's your day going thus far?" Tegene asked.

"It's going. No real complaints to speak about. How about yours?"

"Sooo much better now that I'm talking to you, beautiful." They both chuckled. This was their daily afternoon routine. The couple both own and operate businesses; which can get stressful at times. Tegene owns two tattoo salons as well as being a tattoo artist. Chrisanna is an owner of a fashion stylist coaching practice. Both their businesses are successful, and with success comes the challenges of growing their brands in order to be at the top of their respective industries. There are days when the couple have to deal with the different personalities of their clients; clients who no-show for an appointment, missing ordered shipments. You name it, they both are dealing with it in one form or another.

Their daily afternoon check-ins are another example of the appreciation for the simplicity about their life together. It's their way of being there for each other, it's lending an ear and providing a shoulder to cry on or vent before they see each other at home, because they have a house rule to not bring their work troubles home. Their home is peaceful and sacred ground, their own piece of paradise. The drama-free zone.

"C'Ann, are you still there?" C'Ann is what Tegene calls her.

"Yes, love, I'm still here. Pardon me, what did you say?"

"I asked what should we cook for dinner, or should we go out to dinner?" he asked.

"No, sweetie, let's cook. I'm not in the mood to go out. Let's stay in all weekend... Be totally off the grid. We haven't done that in a while. We'll cook or order takeout, watch movies or not, stay in bed and go half on a baby, or don't do anything at all but be together," Chrisanna stated in a flirty tone.

Chrisanna knew there was a huge, big, all-white teeth smile on Tegene's face by the way his usual deep baritone voice suddenly became a medium falsetto when he agreed, especially about the last part. Off and on for a couple of years, Tegene and Chrisanna had talked about having a baby, and for a few months they tried. When it didn't happen right away, they stopped trying. Oh, Tegene and Chrisanna still get their groove on, they just don't focus on it being to create a baby, but for pure love for each other.

Before Tegene and Chrisanna hung up, they decided to meet up at the local grocery mart to pickup what they will need for their weekend hibernation. Sharing virtual smooches before ending the call. Chrisanna loves her husband and Tegene loves her. She doesn't know how she would survive if she ever lost him. The life she had before Tegene Lexington Madison blew in, was a topsy turvy rollercoaster through a haunted house out the backdoor, falling into a pit of thick molasses tar of emotional and mental quicksand.

At times, Chrisanna didn't know if she would live to see the other side; even as a little girl, there were moments of doubts of ifs, maybes or could-bes. Thirty-three years ago, Chrisanna witnessed a woman murder a man. Testifying about what she saw at eight years old was hard. Police and lawyers, asking her what she saw, what was said and who said it. Where people were standing? Had to talk about her feelings to a strange lady who wrote down every sentence, every word, and every physical action she said and made.

Chrisanna had to go out of state to live with relatives whom she only saw during special family occasions. For years, Chrisanna had to tell her eyewitness story over and over, until one year, she didn't have to tell it no longer, because the woman was granted a compassionate pardon due to health reasons. The woman spent two years in a hospice facility until she died in her sleep. Yet another thing Chrisanna had to eyewitness. The woman was her mother; her mother killed Chrisanna's stepfather during an alcohol and drug fueled physical altercation, of which they had plenty of those during their time together. Chrisanna's mother spent twenty-five years of a life sentence in prison. During that time, she was only allowed to see her mother on holidays, her birthdays, and was allowed phone calls four times a month.

Growing up, Chrisanna had her mindset on not being like her mother; staying in a violent, abusive relationship with a man who faked at loving someone, when all he really loved was himself. For years, Chrisanna would ask her mother how and why she would be with someone like her stepfather. Chrisanna's mother never really gave her an answer, not until a month before she died. Her mother asked her if she remembered her biological father before he passed away from a heart attack. Her mother told her what a wonderful, gentle, kind and loving man he was.

AS WE LAY WITHOUT A CARE

They were high school sweethearts and when Chrisanna's mother got pregnant, they ran away from home, crossed state lines, and got married. They settled in their new state, built a life together, and prepared for the arrival of their beautiful daughter, Chrisanna Arleigh Scott. The seven and a half years as a family were the best years of her mother's life.

When Chrisanna's father died, her mom had a breakdown from the grief. Her mother turned to alcohol to soothe the pain, but never allowed herself to be totally drunk around Chrisanna, because she still had to raise and be strong for her young daughter. Six months after her father's passing, that's when her mother met and married her stepfather. Chrisanna's stepfather was a very charming, smooth talking, GQ-fine dresser who flashed money to mask the fact that he was nothing but a common street hustler, who was an alcoholic and drug addict. He introduced her mother to cocaine and life in the streets. As they drowned heavily in alcohol and drugs, their co-existing became violent and abusive. Chrisanna's mother would have body bruises, blackened eyes and swollen lips for which the explanations didn't make any sense as to how she got them. He too, would have cuts, facial bruises or swollen shut eyes with a ready-made reason on how he got like that. Those were some of the memories Chrisanna remembered until that fateful night. As Chrisanna sat listening to her mother, she had finally realized how a woman who lost the love of her life, succumbed to the toxicity of another man, and watched her whole life disappear with five gunshots.

Chrisanna's heart breaks every time she thinks about her mother and the traumatic events of her life. Her mother's final words to her darling little girl were for Chrisanna to have a better life than she did, find the love of her life, be happy together, and to appreciate each day as if it were their last. Chrisanna gets sad sometimes, because her mother died years before she could meet Tegene, but part of her feels like they did meet and her mother asked God to send Tegene to her baby girl as a gift to make up for everything Chrisanna had to endure growing up; for her mother missing out on Chrisanna's childhood, the loss of her biological father, her mother's years in prison, as well as for her mother's passing.

All these thoughts ran through Chrisanna's mind as she was driving to the grocery mart to meet Tegene. Lord knows she won't be able to thank Him enough for her gift from Him and her mother. Her gift of a loving, kind, intelligent, ambitious man with an awesome sense of humor. Tegene Lexington Madison, devilishly handsome, six-foot eight-inch husband. He towered over other men by a full eight inches. Being a man of dark skin complexion, big and powerful with a sexy, proportioned body; weighing two hundred seventy-five pounds, he carried himself with a commanding air of self-confidence, nonchalant grace, and a smidge of thuggishness.

Pulling into the parking lot, Chrisanna spotted Tegene walking across the lot towards the store, taking notice of his classically handsome features. His profile was sharp and spoke of power with ageless strength. He held his head high with pride which matched his stride. Chrisanna enjoyed looking at this living work of art, especially when he was partially dressed. Tegene was born with God-crafted genes. His chest, broad and muscular, was the perfect background to display the strategically placed assortment of tattoos complemented by very petite, delicate golden circles adorning both of his stiff areolas. Shoulders and biceps structurally outlined as to indicate how much of the world's weight he could carry on any given day. Arms displaying full tattooed sleeves, telling the story of his life thus far. Clothed, partially or fully nude, Tegene's body never disappointed Chrisanna's viewing pleasure. Even in a crowd, his presence was compelling.

After Chrisanna parked her car, she quickly joined Tegene in the store. She texted him to let him know she was in the store and to see which aisle he was in. They met up at the seafood counter. The counter looked dwarfed in front of Tegene. She knew how that felt even though she herself stood exactly six foot tall. Tegene's height towered over her. When people saw them together, Chrisanna wondered if they marveled at the mismatched height and weight between them. His girth was heavier than Chrisanna's. She only weighed, last time she checked, about one hundred eight-five pounds of luscious curves. They greeted each other in their special way, touching their foreheads.

"Finally, you arrived. I was starting to get concerned, but you texted, so all's good now," he stated. She smiled. He should know by now, she would never leave him alone in public for too long; it would be like leaving the door open for the sly foxes to come into the chicken coop. Chrisanna is crazy but not that damn crazy ... please.

Tegene and Chrisanna strolled down the aisles, getting the groceries they thought they would need for tonight's dinner, and for the rest of the weekend meals. They stood in line waiting to check out. Chrisanna felt Tegene's large hand pull her by her waist so that she was standing between him and the shopping cart. He leaned down to whisper in her ear how glad he was at the thought of them being off the grid for the entire weekend and the sexy naughty plans he has for them. All she could do was wickedly smile up at him in agreement as to how much she was pleased he was agreeable to the idea. What Tegene didn't know was Chrisanna, too, had sensually, sinfully good plans for them.

Just as she was about to tease her man with some PDA, she heard a familiar voice call out their names. They both tried not to acknowledge the person, but it was too late; it was Asha Perkins, the homeowners' association president, over in the checkout next to them. Asha asked if she would be seeing them tomorrow for the annual neighborhood potluck jamboree. In unison, they both replied no, because they had other plans at the same time and perhaps next year they would be there. With a disapproving look on her face, Asha turned away from them. Tegene and Chrisanna kinda liked, well, more like tolerated their neighbors in their housing complex during certain times of the year, but they preferred their own company, especially this weekend.

Tegene and Chrisanna spent time together, but they really needed to have quality togetherness. It's what keeps a marriage strong. They checked out. Tegene walked Chrisanna to her car and loaded the groceries in her trunk. He made sure Chrisanna was safely in her car. She drove him over to his SUV. They kissed. Then they raced at a safe speed, of course, to see who would get home first; the loser would cook dinner, of which Chrisanna lost because she got stuck behind a bus picking up passengers. Chrisanna didn't mind losing to her sweetie; it was her turn to cook. Normally on Fridays, Tegene would cook and she would clean up afterwards, but because this weekend was special for them, it was a break from their normal routine.

"Guess someone will be cooking tonight?"

"No fair. I got stuck behind that damn bus, while you took the backroads. Next time, Te. Next time," Chrisanna stated.

"Aww, my poor baby. Life isn't fair. Deal with it my love," Tegene stated as he pulled Chrisanna closer to kiss her on her luscious matte reddish-purple lips.

Taking the groceries and their belongings into their home. Their three fury children, PrettyGirl, Tyson, and Tita; their Rottweiler dogs, greeted them as they walked through the side door into the mudroom. After getting settled in the kitchen, Chrisanna went into their master bedroom to change out of her work attire into more comfy clothes. Sitting on a chair in the corner, Chrisanna began removing her clothing, especially her eighteen-hour constraint to release her twins. Releasing them into freedom until Monday, for which the twins would be grateful.

Walking into their master bathroom, Chrisanna prepared the shower to the temperature she likes, to wash away the day's external stress. Toweling off, Chrisanna applied her newly purchased body lotion of jasmine, rose water mixed with shea butter from Bath & Beyond, to her dampen skin. The fragrance of the lotion was slightly subtle. The lotion gave her skin a smooth, silky-soft touch. Her mind drifted to the last vacation her and Tegene took to St. Croix, Virgin Islands, where the unbelievable sights and rhythmic Caribbean sounds were hypnotic from the time they stepped off the plane. Their resort room overlooked the blueish-greenish turquoise ocean water which seemed to flow until it blended into what looked like an endless horizon of cyan and pale green while waiting for the golden yellow-orange sun to slowly set. The island breeze tickled their noses with a combination of mystical jasmine, perfectly white lilies, Christmas-like red roses with an irrelevant hint of mint and coconut, that fragrant the air around them. A little crooked grin formed on Chrisanna's face as she reminisced. In her mind, it had been a great vacation.

Searching through her basket of fresh laundry for her favorite pair of ripped up shorts and tank t-shirt, she felt Tegene starring at her nude body. She began to blush at the thought of the current view he had while she was bending down. "What a sexy view! I see I came into the room at just the right time," Tegene stated. Looking over her shoulder, Chrisanna gave him a naughty smile and wink.

"Don't get dressed just yet. Give me one more minute before this view disappears under clothing," he pleaded. Chrisanna stood up slowly into what seemed like a graceful, airy, contemporary dancer's pose, twirled, and then walked seductively over to her man. He, like Chrisanna, enjoyed looking at her body. Her beauty spoke volumes of gentle nature, serenely wise, and of overwhelming strength. She was built with a figure that was vivacious, voluptuous-curving, and regal. Her torso was long, full baby-carrying hips, thick thighs and runner's legs. Although, she felt like she could stand to lose a couple of pounds of body weight, Tegene assured her that he was perfectly happy with her weight and that she shouldn't do anything to her body to please him. Chrisanna's weight and height was slightly disproportioned, but she was able to always be stylish, which reflects the effortless look of loving to self-pamper herself weekly, combined with the femininity, confidence, and enchanting allure that most women take years to master, but Chrisanna did it with such ease, always aware of the appreciative glances of which Tegene appreciated as well.

"Darling, I can't stand like this for the rest of the evening. I got to get dressed and get dinner started," Chrisanna stated.

"You know I can't help myself when I see you like this."

"Hmm, you can help it, you just refuse to do so," she said with a giggle in her voice.

As she turned around to put on her clothing, Tegene walked over to her. Wrapping her in his strong, loving arms, they began to slowly sway. She could feel an eager affection coming from him. The prolonged anticipation was almost unbearable for the both of them. Chrisanna leaned her head back onto his chest. She felt the movement of Tegene's breathing and the rhythmic beating of his heart. He placed light kisses on her forehead, then down the side of her neck onto her shoulder. Unapologetically desirable is how Tegene always made Chrisanna feel, even at this moment, it made her feel good and overjoyed to be with him. The joy quickly infected them with the enthusiasm of their overdue weekend together. A delightful shiver of wanting her husband ran through her as his hug got tighter. Tegene swooped her up into his arms. They kissed. Their kissing was as tender and light as a summer breeze, but their irrefutable passion for each other was a blazing flame like a soldering heat that joins metals together.

With a precision-like gesture, Tegene had lowered them onto the closet floor. The plush neutral tone carpet served as the background for what was the start of their growing achiness for lovemaking. Tegene and Chrisanna tried to throttle the dizzying current racing through them. The immediate and total uncontrollable attraction to each other, made Tegene pull her roughly, almost violently into him as she urgingly pushed and pulled his cashmere sweater over his head, then clumsily unbuckled his pants, as a sign of approval to enter into the intimate playground of her body.

Their fingers tingled as they skimmed over each other's skin, and because Chrisanna had just put lotion on her skin, it was extra soft and silky under Tegene's fingertips. Chrisanna used her lips and tongue on

Tegene's piercings to intensify the erotic rhythmic movement between them. Their current emotional wave submerged them in the overflow of a thunderous, intoxicating, climactic ending. Laying there on the floor, the closet's atmosphere had a deep sense of peace and utter amazement. They both remained silent. Neither had expected to start their off the grid weekend this early in the evening; they thought they would wait until after dinner, but sometimes when the moment is right, it's just right. Chrisanna rolled on her side and stared at Tegene who was laying with his eyes closed.

"I can feel you staring. What's wrong, babe?" he asked.

"Nothing's wrong. Just admiring God's gift to me, that's all."

"Well, don't stare too long, we have to get up from here before the dogs come looking for us."

They both chuckled. "Yes, you're right, plus we still haven't eaten." Chrisanna stated.

"Oh, I would say we have eaten already, and it was deliciously out of this world!" he exclaimed. "Ooo-wee, babe, you know you really put an extra oomph on it just now. Whew!"

"Te, you are too silly. But I love you anyway."

"I love you too! Now, let's get up before I dive in for a second and third helping of your good ole lovin'," Tegene stated as he helped Chrisanna off the floor.

They both went into the bathroom to freshen up before heading downstairs. Tegene got the dogs leashed up for their evening walk and Chrisanna went to the kitchen to prepare their dinner. The rest of their evening, they spent eating, laughing, talking, playing with the dogs, basking in their respective afterglow and just enjoying their well-deserved evening alone together. Saturday and Sunday were more of the same.

Each lovemaking moment, more sensually intense than the last. Laying wrapped in each other's arms was cozy, tranquil and tender. The level of their vulnerability with one another grew and it secured their tight bond even further as friends, lovers, and as husband and wife. By Monday morning, neither wanted to go to their respective offices, the emotional mood was just too euphoric to let go, even for a few hours.

    Tegene and Chrisanna made a plan to have more off the grid weekends. Chrisanna thought back on the strange vibe she had felt on Friday and wondered if their weekend mood was it, and not something else strange coming their way. Whatever the vibe was, Chrisanna wasn't going to let it ruin the weekend.

Six weeks later...

"Mr. and Mrs. Madison, thank you for coming in to see me. I have Chrisanna's test results. Chrisanna, congratulations, in seven-and-a-half months, you and Tegene will be new parents of twins," stated the obstetrician.

"OMG!!! What in the what?? How... I mean I know how this happened. I meant to say when did this happen? I thought she had the flu or something. We had given up trying... Just having good 'ole fashioned sex and what not. We didn't expect this, or did we? C'Ann, you aren't saying anything."

"Well, I kinda had my suspicions. I took a home pregnancy test at the office and when it came out positive, I didn't want us to have false hopes like we did previous times. So, I called the doctor, let her do the test, and now it is real. We are going to have a baby... I mean babies. Oh, my Lord," Chrisanna stated as she fainted in the chair.

The joyful news of their soon-to-be arrivals had taken Chrisanna by surprise, but not before she mentally recalled the odd sense from six weeks ago. It was probably her mother preparing her to receive this double blessing she and Tegene have always wanted. "Thank you, Mom!"

"Once in a while, right in the middle of an ordinary life, love gives us a fairy tale." ~ Anonymous

Acknowledgments

I would like to thank all the authors that participated in this anthology. I hope you had a chance to tell your story and be proud of yourself. I hope to work with everyone again in the future.

I want to also thank my family and friends for their support.

To all the readers: Enjoy each story in this book and I hope at least one reader walk away with something. Check out more books on my website written by amazing authors.

Thank you for the support.

Sharnel Williams CEO

Shar-Shey Publishing Co.

www.sharsheypublishingcompany.com

Made in the USA
Columbia, SC
08 March 2020